PUFFIN BOOKS
Editor: Kaye Webb

THE DRAGON'S QUEST

'It's a letter from a shipwrecked sailor!' thought Susan, when she found a corked bottle on the beach with a message inside it. In fact it came from her dear dragon friend, R. Dragon, which was even better.

'Dear Susan,' it said. 'If you come to Constantine Bay this summer I'm afraid you will not find me. I have gone to spend three months with an old friend in the Scilly Isles. I seem to remember that you like good stories, so I have left you, in my cave, a very special book. You will find it on the third rock shelf on the right-hand side.'

Of course, Susan went straight to the cave to find it, and forgetting all about dinner-time, she sat down to read it. It really was the most amazing story, all about how the Cornish princess Guinevere married King Arthur, and took the lucky green dragon with her, how Arthur's wicked half-sister Morgan le Fay worked to destroy the dragon and condemned him to spend a year in the kitchen of Camelot, until finally he was allowed to go on a quest of his own, just like one of the knights, to prove his courage and loyalty.

He set out to find the son of King Jubeance the giant, who had been stolen away as a little boy by a beautiful lady in a big coach, and had never been seen again. It was just the right sort of quest to appeal to the warm-hearted dragon, especially when it dawned on him *who* had taken the child . . .

This exciting story of magic and chivalry fully lives up to the other two Puffin books about friendly, funny R. Dragon: *Green Smoke* and *Dragon in Danger*.

Cover design by Constance Marshall

Rosemary Manning

The Dragon's Quest

ILLUSTRATED BY
Constance Marshall

PENGUIN BOOKS
in association with Longman Young Books

Puffin Books: A Division of Penguin Books Ltd,
Harmondsworth, Middlesex, England
Penguin Books Inc., 7110 Ambassador Road, Baltimore, Maryland 21207, U.S.A.
Penguin Books Australia Ltd, Ringwood, Victoria, Australia
Penguin Books Canada Ltd, 41 Steelcase Road West, Markham, Ontario, Canada

—

First published by Constable 1961
Published in Puffin Books 1974

—

Copyright © Rosemary Manning, 1971

—

Made and printed in Great Britain
by Richard Clay (The Chaucer Press) Ltd,
Bungay, Suffolk
Set in Monotype Garamond

This book is sold subject to the condition
that it shall not, by way of trade or otherwise
be lent, re-sold, hired out, or otherwise circulated
without the publisher's prior consent in any form of
binding or cover other than that in which it is
published and without a similar condition
including this condition being imposed
on the subsequent purchaser

for
ELISABETH ASTLE

Contents

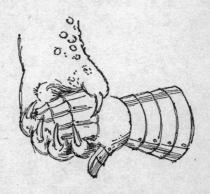

CHAPTER ONE

The Dragon's Letter

THIS chapter is a very short one. It should really have
been called 'Preface' or 'Introduction', but I knew that
you would never read it if I called it by such a boring
name, so I have called it Chapter One. It is written to
explain the rest of the book.

A small girl called Susan used to spend her holidays at
Constantine Bay in Cornwall and had the good fortune
to make friends with a dragon, who lived in a cave on the

beach. Last summer, she went there for the third time and was extremely disappointed to find that the dragon was not in his cave. For several days she searched for him in vain. Then, one morning, wandering along the sands, she found a corked bottle, with what looked like a roll of paper inside it.

It's a message from a shipwrecked sailor! thought Susan, and opened it in much excitement. But it wasn't. It was a letter from the dragon.

Dear Susan [she read]

If you come to Constantine Bay this summer, I'm afraid you will not find me. I have gone to spend three months with an old friend in the Scilly Isles. I seem to remember that you like good stories so I have left you, in my cave, a very special book – the most valuable one in all my library. It is called *The Dragon's Quest*, and tells of my life and adventures at the court of King Arthur. You will find it on the third rock shelf up on the right-hand side, under a flat stone with R.D. scratched on it.

Have a lovely holiday. I am very sorry to miss you, but I have not seen my old friend in the Scilly Isles for seven hundred years and one must keep up with old friends.

Love from
R. Dragon.

Of course, Susan went at once to the cave and climbed up to reach the third shelf. There was the stone marked R.D. and underneath it was a book, just as the dragon had said. Forgetting all about dinner-time, Susan opened the book and began to read.

The Dragon Comes to Court

This is the story of how the dragon came to court, when King Arthur was a young man, and it is the chronicle of that famous quest which in the end brought the dragon his knighthood and an honourable place in the history of the Round Table.

KING Arthur married a beautiful princess of Cornwall, named Guinevere, and the royal wedding took place in London, attended by more than a hundred Cornish knights, who came with the princess from her father's court. With· them came two other splendid gifts, the famous Round Table, and the green dragon who had always gone with the Cornish knights to the wars, blowing out thick clouds of green smoke from his nostrils, and lashing so mightily with his tail that the enemy was mown down like a field of barley at harvest-time. During the wedding festivities the dragon met a strange old woman with a pinched nose and straggling hair, an old woman who, in various disguises, was to play a most important part in this story. To the dragon, the meeting seemed unimportant, but it was, in fact, part of a deep-laid plot in which the King and the dragon himself were to be involved, a plot devised by the King's own half-sister, the wicked Morgan le Fay.

Morgan le Fay was a beautiful woman, and powerful. She practised the arts of magic, but she practised them to no good purpose. She hated her young half-brother,

Arthur, and wished him ill. She desired only that her own husband, King Urience, should be king of all Britain, so that she might have still more power as his queen. She therefore spent her time plotting to bring about the death of Arthur and weaving spell after spell against him.

All her plotting, however, came to nothing, because Arthur himself was both powerful and good, and her spells glanced off him, as a sword slides off a polished shield or breastplate. She was extremely angry when she heard of Arthur's betrothal to Guinevere, for she knew that once he was married, his wife's love would be an added protection to him. So she refused to go to the wedding, and her husband, King Urience, went without her. Alone in her palace at Camelot, however, she was so consumed with curiosity about her brother's new queen and so tempted to cast a spell or two over the pair of them to spoil their happiness, that she went up to London and hid herself, disguised as an ugly old woman, among the crowds. She saw Queen Guinevere and realized at once that though she was beautiful, she was also weak and easily swayed. This delighted Morgan le Fay who knew that mere beauty alone, without goodness, has little power against magic arts and evil spells.

Morgan le Fay sat on the stone steps leading down to the slow-moving Thames, and she thought how best she might waylay Arthur and kill him as he journeyed back to Camelot. She could then crown her husband, Urience, King of Britain and return to Camelot as queen beside him. One afternoon the dragon saw her sitting there. He liked the river and had just dropped into it a corked bottle, with a message for a lobster-catcher friend of his in Cornwall, whom he missed. It read like this:

Dear Harry,

There are no lobsters in the river Thames. I do not know why this is. I am enjoying myself but I miss you and the lobsters.

Your loyal friend,
Dragon.

He watched the bottle as it floated away downstream. The witch Morgan le Fay watched it, too.

'Could you do something for me, a poor old woman?' she croaked.

The dragon looked surprised but he listened to her politely, with his head cocked a little to one side.

'I was too old to stand in the crowds to see the wedding,' she said, 'and I do want to see my br—that noble King Arthur. Would you carry me on your back through the streets and maybe I could catch a glimpse of him?'

The dragon willingly allowed her to ride upon his back, little knowing that he was carrying King Arthur's deadliest enemy. As they went, she questioned him about Arthur, and thus she learnt exactly when he was leaving London, and which route he was taking on his return journey to Camelot. She also learnt that the dragon was going back to Camelot by a different road, and she listened with intense interest to the dragon's tales of his life in Cornwall, and how he brought good fortune in battle to the Cornish knights.

'And you will bring good fortune to that – to King Arthur, too?' she suggested, smiling a twisted smile that the dragon could not see, because she was still perched on his back.

'I trust so,' answered the dragon.

'Never! Never!' hissed Morgan le Fay into the folds of her ragged cloak. 'I will see to that!'

'I beg your pardon?' said the dragon. 'Did you speak?'

'I was asking you to be so kind as to put me down,' croaked Morgan le Fay. She crawled down from the dragon's back, thanked him warmly, and disappeared among the crowd.

Next day, King Arthur and his queen, Guinevere, departed with the knights for their long journey home. The dragon was to travel separately. The King realized that he would be so interested in seeing England and so anxious to climb every hill and dabble in every river, that the journey would take months not weeks. So the dragon was given a special pack-horse, a neat little black beast with white socks, called Starlight, for whom the royal harness-maker made green reins and trappings, embroidered with yellow, to match the dragon's green hide and his yellow claws, horns and scales. He was also given a small escort of Cornish knights, led by Sir Grifflet, who was a friend of his.

They left London on a fine summer morning, with the sun behind them, travelling west towards the King's distant palace of Camelot.

CHAPTER TWO

The Black Forest

Now Morgan le Fay had spent many unhappy and un-
successful hours searching through her volumes of spells
to find one strong enough to be used against King Arthur.
At last she thought that it might be easier to begin by
destroying the dragon, and so, disguised as a croaking
raven, she flapped through the sky, searching for the
dragon's party. At last she spied below her a flash of
silver, which was the armour of his escort, and a flash of
gold, which was, of course, the dragon's horns and fins.

She saw with great interest and delight that they were miles out of their way and obviously lost, also that they were on the very edge of the Kingdom of the Black Forest, which was ruled by a giant called Jubeance. She flew down to a ruined chapel near by, which had once belonged to a hermit, and sat there all night, brooding. The walls were green and slimy with damp. From one window hung a rotten shutter which creaked mysteriously in every gust of wind. The chapel had no roof. Bats flitted in and out over the broken walls, and rats gnawed hungrily at the crumbling wood of an old bench. All these things Morgan le Fay noted with wicked enjoyment, for they put her in the right temper to plot her magic and weave her spells. She sat on a mouldering step and thought about the dragon on whose back she had ridden in the City of London. Once more she had changed her shape, and now she looked every inch a witch, with thin, bony nose, pinched cheeks and glittering eyes.

'The dragon,' she mused aloud. 'The dragon ... he must not reach Camelot. He is a mascot to those Cornish knights. He brings them luck in battle. If he goes with Arthur's knights, they too will be lucky. No one will ever defeat them. Now' – and she drew the word out till it sounded like a howl of the wind – 'N-o-o-o-w, what's to be done?' Her words echoed in the dismal cell. *Be done* ... she heard, and then silence. 'What shall I do next?' *Do next* ... echoed the cold walls.

Morgan le Fay, though strong enough to produce such effects as changes of appearance and changes of place, was not a witch of the first order. Over life itself, she had no power. She could not kill a person by wishing him dead or weaving a spell round him. The most she could do was by her spells to induce another person to act for her. If the dragon was to be destroyed, she knew that she must find someone or something stronger than the dragon to do it for her.

She called to the bats as they flitted past her, but their squeaking replies were too shrill even for her witch ears to catch. She turned impatiently to the dark ground at her feet. There sat a toad, beady-eyed, silent, unmoving.

'Toad!' hissed Morgan le Fay. 'You are old in wisdom. How shall I destroy this dragon?'

The toad blinked his yellow eyes several times and shifted his feet on the cold stone as if he had pins and needles in them. Then he opened his huge mouth and croaked: 'Giant!' *Giant*, echoed the walls softly.

'Which giant, what giant?' demanded Morgan le Fay.

'Giant Jubeance,' croaked the toad, and lowered heavy lids over his yellow eyes.

'I see,' said Morgan le Fay, slowly. 'Giant Jubeance who rules over the land of the Black Forest. Yes, *he* should be strong enough to destroy the dragon, and the stupid creature together with his party of knights will soon be deep into his kingdom. The trouble is, Jubeance is such a good-natured fool. He wouldn't hurt a fly.'

Morgan le Fay sat weaving her fingers in and out of each other.

'Perhaps if I warned the giant in a dream how dangerous the dragon is,' she said at last, 'then when he arrives, the giant will set upon him and kill him.'

She leaned her pointed chin upon her bony hand and stared into the gloomy ivy which covered the wall opposite her. Her eyes never blinked. She sat and stared for a full quarter of an hour. Then she leapt to her feet and wrapping her cloak about her she left the cell and, by her magic power, was far away in no time at all.

That night, before she returned home to her palace in Camelot, a beautiful woman once again, Morgan le Fay prepared her spell. It was a dream which she concocted of herbs and boar's grease, pounded into a paste. She flew to the giant's palace and hovered over his pillow, almost deafened by his snores. She rubbed her dream ointment into his rugged forehead with her fingers. For a long time she made no impression, but at last the ointment began to disappear. Morgan breathed a sigh of relief and returned to her own bed exhausted.

That night, the dragon and his small party slept in a barn on the edge of the giant's kingdom. Next morning, the dragon went out early and looked down the long road with some misgiving. He called Sir Gryfflet and they walked up and down, talking very seriously.

'Gryfflet,' began the dragon, 'I think we're lost.'

'Oh no,' answered the knight, adding rather uncertainly, 'I don't think we can be *lost*. After all, we're going somewhere.'

'Do you happen to know where?' asked the dragon, severely.

'Well, I hope it's Camelot,' said Gryfflet. 'I think we are still going in a westerly direction, aren't we? The sun always seems to be behind us.'

'Gryfflet,' said the dragon, 'does it occur to you that the sun is not always in the same place?'

'Isn't it?' asked Gryfflet, looking alarmed.

'I don't think so,' said the dragon. 'We started in the morning when it was in the east, and we kept it behind us all day. I don't believe we ought to have done that. My bump of geography tells me that we've been walking in loops.'

There was a long silence. Then Gryfflet tried to be encouraging.

'There's the road,' he said. 'It's no good going back the way we've come, so we might as well go forward. It *must* lead somewhere.'

'I don't like it,' said the dragon. 'I'm better with stars than with the sun, and I suggest we wait here all day, and I will work out our direction by the Pole Star tonight. I'm used to stars. We have a lot of them in Cornwall.'

But the escort thought this a great waste of time. They all lost their tempers over it and in the end they set out down the road, and the dragon refused to speak a word to anyone all day.

Meanwhile, in his vast and gloomy castle, the giant had been dreaming Morgan le Fay's dream. He dreamed that a dreadful dragon destroyed many of his people and his flocks. This dragon had come flying out of the west and his head, so it seemed to the giant, was like green enamel, smooth and shining; his fins glittered like gold and his claws were bright yellow. A hideous flame of fire streamed out of his mouth. He burnt up the fields as he came.

The giant woke up in a cold sweat of fear. Like many very large creatures, he was really rather timid and easily frightened, and as soon as he woke from his dream, he clutched his wife's shoulder and bellowed: 'Martha! Martha! I've had a terrible nightmare!' With that he burst into tears.

His wife patted him kindly and said: 'There, there, tell me all about it, dear.'

'I dreamt – I dreamt –' blubbered the giant, mopping his eyes with the sheet, 'I dreamt a horrible dragon came flying over our country, breathing out flames, and destroying everything.'

'Never mind,' said the giant's wife, soothingly. 'It was only a dream.'

'No, no,' cried the giant. 'It will come true. It is a terrible warning. We shall all be destroyed! Our kingdom will be ruined! Oh, Martha, what shall we do?'

'Don't be silly, dear,' said Martha, firmly. 'You've forgotten something very important. A dream that's told before eight o'clock in the morning always turns out the opposite way. Now, if you'd been stupid enough to hide your dream from me, then you *would* have something to fear, but as it is – why, you needn't worry at all. If a dragon does come here, he'll turn out to be a friendly one, and will probably catch some sheep for you to have for dinner. You'll see.'

The giant became calmer, for he knew his wife was generally right, and any lingering fears he had quickly flew away when he heard the castle clock chime eight o'clock.

'I told you just in time,' he said, beaming.

All that day, the dragon and his small company had trudged down the rather rough road leading into the giant's domain. In the late afternoon, a large forest came into sight far ahead of them.

'You know,' said Sir Gryfflet, 'I don't think this *can* be right. It looks to me,' he added nervously, 'like the land of Black Forest. I've heard of that. They say it is ruled over by a giant.'

The dragon snorted and plodded crossly on. 'It was not I who insisted on coming,' he muttered. 'I knew we ought to have waited till nightfall and taken our bearings from the stars, but no notice was taken of me. Oh, no! My bump of geography was ignored by you all.'

The company of knights looked very uncomfortable. The sky was now overcast. Dark clouds were gathering on the horizon, where they hung heavily over the black forest which they were approaching. Cloud and forest grew darker and darker until it was impossible to tell which was which. Sir Gryfflet was shivering, but the dragon walked steadily on, with his jaws tightly clenched. Suddenly there was a flash of lightning, followed by a deep drum-roll of thunder. The clouds above the forest folded back like curtains and revealed, standing up on the skyline, the outlines of a gigantic castle. The whole party stopped in its tracks.

'I can hardly believe,' said the dragon, 'that those are the towers of Camelot.'

'They are not, indeed,' said Sir Gryfflet. 'They are nothing like them. It must be the giant's castle.'

All of them were beginning to fear that Sir Gryfflet's words were true, when suddenly, amid rolls of thunder and bright flashes of lightning, they saw a man hurrying towards them down the road from the forest. He was on horseback, fully armed, and was at least eight feet high. Sir Gryfflet's knees shook so much that his armour clattered noisily, and the dragon told him quite angrily to pull himself together.

'He'll kill us all!' shouted one of the knights, as the rider came galloping down the road.

'Fly, fly!' cried another.

The bodyguard waited no longer. They fled, and were well away within a few seconds, Sir Gryfflet turned to follow them, but the dragon seized him by the belt, hooking one claw through it and pulling him back.

'Sir Grylflet,' said the dragon, sternly. 'Do you or do you not wish to be made a member of King Arthur's Round Table?'

'I do, I do,' snuffled Sir Grylflet, almost in tears.

'Then be a man,' said the dragon, 'and I will be a dragon, and between us we will withstand the enemy, no matter what size he is.'

By this time the eight-foot knight was very near indeed, but before he quite reached them he pulled up his horse in a cloud of dust and shouted: 'I come in peace and friendship. My master welcomes you, if you are friends. If not, declare yourselves now and depart from the Black Forest.'

'The Black Forest?' stammered poor Sir Grylflet. 'Oh, let me go, Dragon, or we shall be eaten alive.'

'Nonsense,' retorted the dragon. 'No one can eat me. Far too scaly. He'd choke. Let me answer him.' He cleared his throat noisily. 'We are friendly travellers on our way to Camelot,' he said. 'Who is your master?'

'King Jubeance, the giant,' came the reply. 'You may have heard of him.'

'We have,' muttered Sir Grylflet.

'I haven't,' said the dragon. 'I come from Cornwall and I never heard of Giant Jubeance in my life. However, I am well used to giants, since we had plenty in Cornwall, until I got rid of them –' and at that the dragon fixed the armed bodyguard very fiercely with his eye. 'You can't frighten me with giants.'

The tall knight smiled quite pleasantly. 'King Jubeance is most anxious to meet you – if you come in friendship, of course. He has had a dream about you.'

'A dream?' repeated the dragon, rather flattered that anyone should dream about him. 'What did I do?'

'He will tell you himself if you will do him the honour of waiting upon him in his castle.'

'It's a trap,' muttered Gryfflet into the dragon's ear.

'Stuff and nonsense!' answered the dragon. 'I want to meet him, and this noble fellow wants an answer to his master's very civil invitation. I propose that we accept.'

'All right,' said Gryfflet, uneasily.

'Sir,' called the dragon to the tall knight, whose horse was getting restive, and pawing the ground. 'Tell your master we are graciously pleased to accept his invitation.'

The knight wheeled his horse round and galloped back towards the dark forest, in the midst of which loomed the towers of the castle of the Giant Jubeance. There was a moment's silence, and then the two travellers followed him.

CHAPTER THREE

The Castle

THE dragon plodded ahead firmly, with Gryfflet trailing unwillingly a little way behind him. At last the knight said gloomily: 'I wonder what's happened to the others?'

'Probably eaten by another giant,' remarked the dragon heartlessly. Gryfflet shivered.

The sky had cleared now, and the clouds were disappearing over the horizon. As they entered the forest a deep silence descended upon them. The heavy feet of the dragon and the iron-shod hooves of Gryfflet's horse made no sound on the soft carpet of pine needles. There was a clear track between the trees and above it could be seen the sky, like a thin blue ribbon, but on either side the forest was so thick that it shut out the light, and the two travellers felt as though night had already fallen upon them. Gryfflet's discomfort and fear was shown by his frequent sighs.

The dragon, who did not like the forest either but was determined not to show his inner alarm, at last turned round on the knight and said, 'Do for goodness' sake stop sighing. It makes me think there's a bear or an elephant or something lurking in the trees.'

'There probably is,' said Gryfflet, miserably.

'Well, let's frighten it, then,' said the dragon, briskly, and with that he blew several huge puffs of smoke to right and left which billowed under the trees, weaving among the crowded trunks like a green mist. The dragon then shook his scales and the noise reverberated through the silences with terrible effect, so that everything which heard it slipped hastily away into its burrow or hole or nest and lay there quaking.

'There's the castle!' cried the dragon, suddenly, pointing ahead. He felt sorry for Grypflet, and also perhaps a little sorry for himself, for they had only the word of the tall knight that the giant was a friendly one. He stopped and took Grypflet's mailed hand in his own green paw.

'Dragons Never Despair!' he cried, as boldly as he could.

'A Grypflet's grip never lets go!' echoed the knight, dismounting and feeling considerably braver after the dragon's heartening words.

With that the two adventurers strode up to the huge door which towered above them. It was made of thick oak and studded with nails as big as a man's fist, and was opened by the same tall knight who had ridden through the forest to meet them earlier. Lined up behind him were nine others, equally tall. The dragon bristled and blew out a small puff of green smoke. He also lifted his paws rather high in the air as he walked up the steps in order to show how large his claws were. Grypflet followed him, his knees knocking together.

The dragon cast a swift look behind him. 'Dragons Never Despair,' he whispered.

'A Grypflet's grip –' quavered the Cornish knight.

A little uncertainly, they began to walk between the lines of tall armed men, and as they did so, the great door was shut fast behind them, and they found themselves in the hall of the castle. The roof was of blackened oak beams, roughly carved with the figures of beasts and birds.

The walls were of grey stone, and at one end a flight of wide steps led from the hall to the upper storey. Straight ahead of the dragon and Gryfflet was an archway, leading into some room beyond. It was heavily curtained with a great hanging made of sheepskins, sewn together. At intervals round the walls hung the antlers of deer, and the horns of cattle, while over the stone flags of the floor had been flung a number of animal skins, brown oxen, red-spotted deer, and the black bristly wild boar. It was obviously the hall of a mighty hunter and eater of meat.

Before they had time to do more than glance at all this, however, one of the knights cried in a thundering voice: 'His Majesty, King Jubeance!'

The sheepskin curtain was held aside and through the arch came an enormous figure. The dragon, being a large creature himself, was not perhaps so impressed by his size as was poor Sir Gryfflet, but even the dragon had to push with his paws very firmly into the deerskin on which he was standing, to prevent his legs from trembling. The giant had a large round red face, not at all ill-humoured, a shock of red hair, and large clumsy hands, one of which held an immense drinking-horn. He stopped under the archway for a moment and gazed at his two visitors. Then his face broke into a vast grin. He tossed his drinking-horn behind him with a clatter, and advanced with hand outstretched.

'I'm right glad to see you,' he cried, in a voice that filled the whole hall. 'It's not often that I get a chance to meet anyone of my own size. You're very welcome!'

With that, he shook the dragon's paw vigorously, and then suddenly noticed Gryfflet.

'Is that boy your page?' he asked.

'Not exactly,' answered the dragon. 'He is Sir Gryfflet

of Cornwall, a knight of high repute, appointed by King Arthur to be my escort.'

'Then he's welcome too!' roared Jubeance and stooped down to give poor Grywflet a handshake that pulled him into the air and dropped him down again, a dozen feet away, with all the breath knocked out of his body.

'Now, I'm an honest man,' cried the giant, 'and I won't deceive you. I had a terrible dream last night – of a huge dragon that came into my kingdom to eat up my land and my people. But I told the wife about it in the morning, and d'you know what she said? "Jube," says she. "A dream that's told early enough always turns out t'other way round. This dragon of yours will be a friendly beast and bring you nothing but good".'

'Your wife,' said the dragon, relieved, 'is a pearl of wisdom. I look forward to meeting her.'

Grywflet was speechless and could only bow.

'Follow me,' said the giant, and led the way under the

arch into another hall, down the centre of which was a long table laid for dinner. The tall knights came in and took their places behind ten chairs. The dragon and Gryfflet were placed one at each end, and a moment later the giant's wife entered from the kitchen, slipping off an apron as she came, her face very red with the heat of cooking.

'I hope you gentlemen will excuse me,' she said, cheerfully, 'but cook is that contrary this evening, and when she's in one of her tizzies nothing is right if I don't see to it myself. Bless me, if she hadn't forgotten the dumplings and I only just got 'em in in time!'

She shook hands with the dragon and Gryfflet and everybody sat down. In came the servants, bearing a pot as big as a barrel which they set down in front of the giant. He stood up and seized a ladle like a saucepan.

'Stew?' he queried, raising his red, bushy eyebrows.

'Stew!' said his wife. 'The best ever and full of meat.'

The dragon coughed nervously. 'I hate to make a fuss,' he said, 'but I don't really care for meat. Would you – would you pick me out the vegetables and the – er – the dumplings. I'm very partial to dumplings.'

The giant gazed dumbfounded at the dragon. 'Not – eat – meat?' he bellowed.

'Not really, if you don't mind,' said the dragon. 'It's a long story. I won't go into it now, but it's a – a kind of vow. I have promised not to eat it.'

The tall knights were all gazing at the dragon in astonishment.

'You really mean it?' asked the giant, as he fished in the bowl of stew for dumplings and carrots and onions and turnips.

'I really do,' said the dragon, though he licked his lips,

and gazed rather wistfully at the steaming pot, while his nostrils twitched.

When everyone was served, King Jubeance took a few mouthfuls, sighed with satisfaction and sat back. 'Sir Dragon,' he began, 'I never met a vegetarian before. I want to know why you, a dragon with good teeth and a good appetite' (the dragon had nearly cleared his plate already), 'don't eat meat. So out with the tale, and it will make the meal the merrier.'

The dragon paused to dip a wedge of bread into his gravy, and after swallowing this with obvious enjoyment, wiped his mouth on a handkerchief and said, solemnly, 'Ten years ago, Your Majesty, I took a vow to keep off meat, as far as possible. I had been a wicked dragon. I had eaten not only huge quantities of cattle, sheep, pigs and poultry, but – I hate to say it – I had eaten several maidens.'

'What of it?' cried Jubeance. 'I've eaten several myself in my youth. I hated doing it, but what else can we huge creatures do? We've got to live, same as other people.'

'Have you never thought,' said the dragon, laying down his knife and fork, 'have you never thought of the sorrow you are bringing on the fathers and mothers of those poor maidens you've eaten up?'

At the far end of the table, the kindly Martha burst into loud sobs and cried: 'Oh, I did tell him! I told him over and over again, but he gets so hungry, he can't resist them, and it does make him so unpopular with his people. It's bad enough when he takes all their beef and mutton, but the next time he eats a *person* there'll be a revolution –'

'Go on with your story,' interrupted the giant, looking rather cross.

'I'll cut it short,' said the dragon, 'for I don't wish to be tedious and keep the next course waiting. I once had a thorn in my paw. No one would help me for they hated and feared me, but at last a holy man, called Petroc, pulled the thorn out and healed my paw, and in return I promised him I would never eat meat of any kind again.'

Jubeance looked at the dragon, open-mouthed with surprise. At this moment, Martha appeared with a great platter of jam tart, and for a time no one said anything at all.

At last the dragon wiped his sticky mouth delicately with his handkerchief (a piece of good manners which drew an approving smile from the motherly Martha), and said, 'Have you ever thought of porridge?'

'Porridge?' repeated the giant. 'Why should I think of it?'

'To eat, I mean,' went on the dragon.

'What is it?' asked Jubeance. 'It sounds like cattle food.'

'It is, in a way,' said the dragon. 'It's made of oats and water, boiled.'

The giant looked horrified. 'It sounds disgusting.'

'You add sugar and milk,' said the dragon, soothingly, 'and it fills you up. The knights of Scotland eat very little else, I understand. Every knight goes into battle with a lance, a shield, and a bag of oats slung over his saddle, to make porridge with.'

The giant looked interested. 'They actually *fight* on nothing but porridge?'

'They do, so I heard from a Scottish dragon I once knew,' said the dragon. 'Hamish MacDragon, his name was, and he ate a wash-tub full of porridge every morning and told me it lasted him until quite five o'clock, when he had a light snack of a sheep or a couple of turkeys, or something like that – nothing much.'

'I do wish you'd try it, dear,' said Martha, kindly.

The giant became silent. He offered second helpings all round, but the dragon noticed that he absent-mindedly buttered his own piece of jam tart and put a large piece of cheese on it, as though it were a biscuit.

When dinner was over, the giant produced a black bottle of wine from a corner cupboard. 'You'll take a little for your health, my dear?' he said to his wife.

'I think I will, Jube, just tonight,' answered Martha.

Jubeance poured out some wine in a glass as big as a mixing bowl. 'Now, Sir Dragon, you and your friend Gryfflet will partake, I hope?'

'We'll be delighted,' said the dragon.

'Just a drop,' said Gryfflet. 'The glasses are rather large.'

'Use my thimble,' suggested Martha, and fished in her pocket. 'Here it is.' She held up a silver thimble the size of a wine glass.

'Thank you,' said Gryfflet, gratefully. 'That will do very well.'

They sat round the great stone hearth in the giant's hall, chatting very pleasantly as they sipped their wine.

'How unexpected this is,' remarked the dragon, leaning back in his great chair, and crossing his legs. The bright fire in the hearth caught his golden horns and fins and he looked very handsome, with his wine glass held in one elegant paw, while the other waved gently to and fro as he talked. 'We never thought, did we, Sir Gryfflet, as we made our way through that dark forest this morning, that we should be sitting with you, Your Majesty, and with your excellent wife, drinking a friendly glass, and talking like old friends?'

'We did not,' said Gryfflet, shuddering a little, as he thought how terrible that ride had been, earlier in the day.

'Ha, ha, ha!' laughed the giant. 'Such silly tales are told of giants. We are harmless, home-loving people, aren't we, Martha?'

'We are, Jube,' said his wife and squeezed her husband's hand affectionately.

'And have you any children?' answered the dragon, by way of conversation.

At these words, a dreadful thing happened. The giant's wife burst into tears and buried her face in a vast handkerchief. Gryfflet was extremely embarrassed and gazed steadily into the fire. The dragon coughed and shuffled his paws.

'There, there,' said Jubeance, patting his wife. 'It's all right, old girl.'

'Tell them, Jube,' sobbed Martha. 'Tell them everything.'

The giant wiped away a tear himself, and clearing his throat, which seemed to have gone husky, said: 'My friends, we have – we had – a son. Our only child. We called him Giles. For three years that boy was the light of our eyes and the joy of our hearts. And then, one day, his nurse took him for a walk through the trees, right down as far as the highway. She was a silly girl and wanted to meet her sweetheart who was a farm lad just the other side of the forest. She and the boy were talking, when a great coach drove past, and came to a stop. Out leans a beautiful lady. "That's a fine boy," she calls out. "Oh," says the girl, hardly looking, for she only had eyes for her farm lad, "oh, yes, he's a well-grown child, ain't he?" "How old is he?" asks the lady. "Three, Your Lady-ship," answers the girl. "My, but he's well-grown for three!" says the stranger, then. "Oh well, ma'am, he's a giant's son, you see." Now the girl *says* she never took her eyes off our Giles and that he just vanished into thin air, like a puff of smoke.'

'But we know what happened,' interrupted Martha, 'for the farmer's boy told us himself later. She turned to whisper and giggle with him, and in a trice, that wicked woman had nipped out of the coach, and picked our Giles up. She was back in the coach next minute, and driving away. We never saw him again.'

With that the poor Queen burst into further sobs. The dragon was very upset. 'I'm sorry I mentioned it,' he said, and patted her hand kindly. 'To kidnap a child,' he said, gravely, 'would be an offence that our noble King Arthur would never allow to go unpunished. Who was this wicked woman? Did you never find out?'

'Never,' said the giant, heaving a sigh. 'The girl was too silly to take anything in, and she stuck to her story that he had vanished like smoke. The only clue we had was a chance remark by the farmhand. He said he noticed the coat of arms on the side of the coach. It was three cooking-pots, he said. Black ones. But there, it was no use. We never traced whose arms they were. I expect it was his invention. It's years ago now. Ah, yes, my boy would be nearly twenty now.'

The dragon, who was a tactful creature, changed the subject. 'What a pleasant castle you have here,' he said brightly, looking round the great hall. 'Very cosy. A real home.' And he began to describe the comforts of the cave in which he lived in Cornwall. At last, however, they all grew sleepy and the giant began to yawn.

'Time for bed!' he cried, and Martha lit a candle and took the knight and the dragon off to the spare room of the castle, where Sir Gryfflet went to sleep in a four-poster bed, and the dragon stretched out on the soft rugs of the floor.

Early the next morning, they set out on their journey to Camelot, fortified by a double-size breakfast cooked by Martha, and a map of the route sketched by the kindly giant king.

CHAPTER FOUR

Camelot

BY this time Morgan le Fay, who kept her spies in every castle, had learned that her plot had gone wrong. Far from slaying the dragon, the giant had made friends with him. This was a sad blow to Morgan le Fay. It may seem strange that a sorceress could not do exactly as she wished, but as I've said there was a good reason why she was seldom able to do as much evil as she intended: her magic powers were not of a strong kind. She had learned them, such as they were, from an old Cornish nurse she had had when a child. This woman had been employed at the castle of Tintagel to look after the King's daughters. Little Morgan le Fay was her favourite, for in her she saw a willing pupil ready to lap up magical knowledge, and it was a great grief to the nurse when she found that all Morgan wanted to do with her magic arts was to harm others. 'Very well, then,' she said, 'before I go too far, I'll see that it is only paltry little spells that I teach you. Then, if you wish to bring about anything worse, like a sickness or a death, you won't have power to do it!'

That is why Morgan le Fay was powerless to do any

great magic, and had to make others work for her if she wanted something important to be done.

Having now learnt of the failure of her dream charm, she was casting about in her mind for another idea. She still had some of the charm left in the box, and she was loath to waste it, for her magic was too precious to her to be thrown away, half-used, 'I will try it out on Arthur,' she said to herself, for the King and Queen and all the court were now back at Camelot, and Urience and Morgan le Fay had a palace themselves, near by, and often spent the evening with Arthur and Guinevere.

It chanced that one evening at dinner the King complained of a headache. Morgan le Fay noticed him leaning his forehead wearily in his hands, so she withdrew from the table, flew home, and came back with her precious box of dream magic.

'Dear brother,' she said, 'if you would but rub this on your brow, your pain would vanish overnight. It is a soothing herbal balm. I beseech you to give it a trial.'

But Arthur pushed it away. He hated to admit that anything was the matter with him. 'It's nothing at all,' he said, 'Don't make a fuss, sister.'

However, Morgan was not one to give up easily. She handed the charm to Queen Guinevere and whispered, 'Rub it on his forehead tonight when he is asleep. It will cure his aching head.' Then she added as an afterthought: 'And bring him *sweet dreams* as well.'

Guinevere promised gratefully to do this, for she had no idea, as indeed no one had, of Morgan le Fay's secret hopes and plots. That night she rubbed the dream charm upon Arthur's forehead. He slept very restlessly, tossing about a good deal and once or twice crying out in his sleep. When he woke in the morning, he looked dazed.

'I have had a very strange, a very disturbing dream,' he muttered.

'Tell me, my dearest,' urged Guinevere.

But the dream had been about a dragon and the King did not like to tell his wife, who had come from Cornwall and loved the dragon. Instead, he called to him one of his best loved knights, Gawaine, who happened also to be his nephew.

'I have dreamt a strange dream, nephew,' said the King. 'I dreamt that a dreadful dragon came flying out of the west. His shoulders shone like gold and his tail was long and scaly. His claws were like gold, too, and fearsome flames of fire flowed out of his mouth. This dragon devoured many of the people, and brought a terrible destruction over my land.'

Sir Gawaine did not believe, as the giant's wife did, that if you tell a dream early enough it will turn out the opposite way. He took the dream very seriously, and gave Arthur this advice: 'This must be a warning. When the dragon arrives at court, get rid of the Cornish knights, send them out to – to hunt, anything to get them out of the way. Then I and my Scots knights will soon put an end to this creature for you.'

Arthur did not like Gawaine's idea at all for he had seen no harm in the dragon; but he was afraid of his dream. In the end, he reluctantly took the Scotsman's advice and told him to make the necessary arrangements.

'But no killing,' he said. 'Just get rid of the dragon. Send him back to Cornwall, or better still, send him under escort to Wales, and lose him in the Black Mountains.'

Gawaine pretended to agree, but secretly he thought it would be far better if the dragon were killed and then there would be no danger of any trouble with him in the future.

A few days after this, as the King and some of his knights were walking one morning on the high battlements of the castle at Camelot, discussing affairs of state, they saw a faint haze of green smoke rising from the distant horizon. At first none of them knew what it was. Then someone cried: 'It must be the green dragon that came with the Round Table from Cornwall! He blows green smoke.'

A cloud passed over the King's face. Then he turned away and went slowly down the stone spiral staircase to the great hall of the castle. He called Gawaine to him. 'The dragon is coming,' he said, quietly. 'Do as I ordered you.'

Now Gawaine had a great deal to do before the dragon arrived. He had to call the Cornish knights together, and persuade them to go off hunting, whether they wanted to or not. Then he had to collect his own Scotsmen together with their weapons in the courtyard, ready to fall upon the dragon as soon as he arrived. Meanwhile Arthur, who felt extremely uneasy about the whole matter and had no wish to see what happened, had planned to sit in the solar with the Queen and play chess, partly to prevent her from noticing anything, and partly to occupy his own attention. He felt guilty and did not wish to think about his order to Gawaine.

All these plans were overthrown, however, by something which neither Arthur nor Gawaine had foreseen. The dragon and Sir Gryfflet, after travelling for several days, had at last reached a high hill, some ten miles or so away from Camelot, and it was here that the dragon had blown out several puffs of green smoke, the very ones

which had been seen by Arthur and his knights. The
dragon and Grysslet sat quite a long time on top of this
hill, partly to recover their breath after the climb, and
partly to admire the splendid view. Ahead of them
stretched a wide plain, threaded by silver rivers. Shining
like tiny mirrors in the dark green carpet of the plain lay
three still lakes. In the far distance were hills, wooded and
blue.

'This,' said the dragon, 'is a beautiful prospect. We
have no such country as this in Cornwall, have we,
Grysslet?'

'We have cliffs and rocks,' said the Cornish knight,
reproachfully.

'True, true,' answered the dragon, 'but it's pleasant
to have a change. I look forward to living at Camelot, at
least for a time. I presume that *is* Camelot, that small grey
dot in the centre of the plain?'

'That is it,' answered Grysslet.

'I have a sudden desire to fly,' announced the dragon.
'I have not stretched my wings for some months, and I
would like also to give them a pleasant surprise at
Camelot. If they have seen my green smoke, they will
know that we shan't be among them for at least half a
day, but I could fly there in a few minutes.'

'I can't fly,' said Grysslet.

'I will take you on my back,' said the dragon.

'What about my horse?' asked Grysslet.

'I can't take him,' replied the dragon. 'But from here,
he can easily find his own way back. I am told horses have
an excellent sense of direction.'

Somewhat unwillingly, for he had never flown before,
Sir Grysslet climbed upon the dragon's back. It was the
first and last time he flew, and he never forgot it. The

wind whistled through his helmet with a high whining sound. Below him, the land unfolded quickly, like a roll of patterned cloth – rivers, lakes, woods, fields and farms. And then – there were the grey towers of Camelot, and a swarm of men like bees assembling in the courtyard. These men were, of course, the Cornish knights, being rounded up by Gawaine, ready to be sent off on their day's hunting.

The dragon's decision to fly had wrecked Gawaine's plans. The Cornish knights had not even finished assembling, let alone set out, and his own Scotsmen had neither been summoned together nor armed, when suddenly, there was the dragon, landing on the green sward of the bailey of the castle, all smiles and puffs of green smoke, and paw-shakes all round, while Sir Gryfflet, a trifle pale and bewildered, and with the plumes blown right off his helmet, scrambled off his back. The Cornish knights clustered round them, laughing and shouting for joy, in their curious Cornish language, which, of course, the dragon and Gryfflet could understand.

Gawaine came out into the courtyard and was very put-out to discover what was happening. Behind him clattered some of the Scottish knights, buckling on their armour and pushing their helmets over their heads. When they saw that the Cornish knights were still there and the dragon as well, they did not know what to do. Gawaine did not dare tell them to attack the dragon in the presence of his Cornish friends.

'You'd better go back to the armoury and wait,' he said. 'Maybe there'll be nothing to do today.'

Word had now reached King Arthur that the dragon had arrived unexpectedly. He strode quickly down to the courtyard and a silence fell among the knights when he appeared. The dragon bowed low, and made a short speech.

'Your Majesty,' he began. 'I and my escort, Sir Grы-fflet, having braved many a danger and undergone hardships of every kind, have at last arrived at your court. The rest of my escort, cowardly fellows, fled away as soon as we encountered danger, and I hope Your Majesty will deal with them as they deserve. Sir Grуfflet alone stayed by my side. I have brought him through the air for the last ten miles, so eager was I to see again my royal master.'

Here the dragon bowed again. He then looked up at the King and was surprised to see no welcoming smile upon the royal face.

'Dragon,' said the King, at last. 'How long is it since you ate anyone?'

The dragon was indignant. 'At least twenty years, Your Majesty.'

'But you still have strong teeth,' said the King, 'and sharp ones. How do I know that you will not be a danger to my people?'

There were indignant murmurings among the Cornish knights, but the King stilled them with his hand.

'Listen, my good Cornishmen! And you, green dragon of the western coasts. I have dreamed a strange dream and a dream is not sent into one's mind for nothing. My counsellor Merlin taught me to take heed of dreams. Dragon, I cannot trust you. I dare not keep you in my kingdom, after this dream. You are a danger to my people. I might have had you destroyed, but that I will not do. I command you only – leave my kingdom and do not return to it.'

At this, the mutterings of the Cornish knights grew to

a loud clamour. Angrily they clustered round the dragon. There were cries of: 'Let us return to Cornwall! We will take the Round Table with us! Ungrateful king!'

Yet the oldest and wisest of them all called them to silence and begged them to listen to him. 'My friends,' he said, 'it is not easy for the King to do this. Remember that we Cornishmen, too, believe that there is truth in dreams. The King is young. He wishes to rule over a peaceful and contented kingdom. He is right to take heed of his dreams. Do not blame our noble King, and you, O Dragon, accept your fate. The King is being merciful. He might have had you destroyed, but he asks you to depart. With deep sorrow we shall see you go, but the King must be obeyed. Return to Cornwall, O Dragon, return and live as you once lived on the rocky shores of our coast, and one day when the King has forgotten his dreams, perhaps you will come back to us.'

After this speech, many of the Cornishmen were in tears and others were looking angry and fingering their swords. The dragon had turned away and slowly, with heavy, sorrowful feet, had begun to go, his noble head drooping, his tail dragging along the ground.

But suddenly there was a cry, and there in the courtyard was the Queen. She flung herself upon her knees before the King, and begged him to hear her. 'My royal husband,' she began, 'do not send our dragon away from the court. Are you not Cornish, too? Your father was Uther Pendragon of Cornwall, and bore a dragon's name. A flaming dragon appeared in the sky at your birth. The dragon brings good fortune to Cornishmen. Do not send him away.'

'I must obey my dream,' said the King.

'Give him a year,' begged the Queen. 'He has come

all this way with us and he is a noble beast. If you send him away, many of the Cornish knights will go with him, and I, your queen, will be brought into much sorrow.'

The King hesitated. 'What shall I do then?' he asked, in a low voice.

The Queen rose from her knees. 'A month ago,' she said, 'there came a young man to your court who refused to give his name. You sent him to your kitchens to serve there for a year, to test his endurance. Do the same with the dragon.'

The King still hesitated. The dragon turned and fixed him with his sad, yellow eyes. 'O King!' he said. 'Do as the Queen asks. Send me to the kitchens. There I shall be in the midst of plenty: fat joints of meat all round me, hanging from hooks in the ceiling, bubbling in the cauldrons, sizzling in the ovens. Yet if I so much as lick my tongue round a piece of gristle, may I be banished from your kingdom for ever. Will this break the power of your dream?'

The King was at heart a merciful and just man. 'Very well,' he said, at last. 'I will grant the Queen's wish.'

A sigh of relief went round and as the King turned to go, the dragon spoke again. 'At the end of the year, will you grant me a gift, O King?'

'I will,' replied Arthur. 'If you keep your vow, I will grant you a boon. Lead him away to the kitchens.'

The dragon knew that Arthur was not angry with him. Indeed, the King looked at him with love as he plodded slowly away. But all of us must obey and accept what is sent us by the powers which surround us, be they the powers of magic, the spells of the faery folk or the warnings of dreams.

CHAPTER FIVE

The Kitchens

WHEN the dragon reached the kitchens, he sat down before a large fire, in front of which were roasting at least twenty geese. The birds went round and round on long iron spits, fat dripping from them. A dirty little boy in a greasy leather apron worked the spit, turning it round slowly with a handle, and as soon as he saw the dragon, he said, 'I yeard o' you.'

'So I should hope,' said the dragon, with dignity. 'I am a famous animal.'

'Famous, are yer?' said the turnspit. 'Yer just a bad dream, that's what you are.'

The dragon made no reply to this insolence.

'Wouldn't you like a goose?' went on the boy.

'No,' replied the dragon, looking away from the succulent, dripping birds. 'No, I do not happen to like meat.'

'Go on,' said the young limb. 'Tell that to the butchers!'

The dragon closed his eyes and took no notice. He thought: I can see plainly that this year is going to be

hard to bear. In the first place, I *do* like meat. And to see
it all round me and not eat even the smallest morsel is
going to try my patience and self-control to the uttermost
limit. Then there is the sadness of parting from my
friends – the Cornish knights, Queen Guinevere, my dear
stupid old Grynflet. I shall not see them for a whole year.
At this the dragon's eyes began to fill with tears. But he
was determined not to show his feelings in front of the
turnspit so he swallowed hard and thought of something
else.

I must have a useful year, he thought. I must learn to
cook. Or perhaps I might learn a new language. One of
the cooks might be a foreigner. Then there is Giles. I must
plan my search for Giles. Yes – the dragon suddenly
opened his eyes and looked fiercely at the turnspit, who
quailed – that shall be my quest when I leave these
kitchens in twelve months' time – the quest for Giles.

'Yah!' said the turnspit, trying to get a rise out of the
dragon.

'You had better watch the spit,' said the dragon, coldly.
'The second bird from the end is burning.' With that
he turned away and started to walk through the kitchen.

'Mind out!' called a cheerful voice, and the dragon
suddenly saw a large black cooking-pot just above his left
eye. He backed away and found himself looking up into
the face of a smiling fair-haired scullion. 'You're over
large even for these kitchens,' said the young man and
hurried on.

Here at last is a friendly face, thought the dragon,
wondering who the young man was. Meanwhile he
looked about him and explored the kitchens as best he
could without getting in the way of the scullions and
cooks and carvers and servers.

In charge of the whole kitchen department was Sir Kay, uncle of King Arthur, a bad-tempered, ill-mannered man who had never recovered from his disappointment when Arthur and not his own son pulled the magic sword out of the stone, and so became King of England. The dragon took an instant dislike to him.

'Note 1,' said the dragon to himself, taking out a small notebook. 'Growl at Sir Kay as often as possible.'

Later he added two more notes, in a small, careful handwriting.

'Note 2. Keep out of the roasting kitchen, meat too tempting and turnspits too insolent.'

'Note 3. Find out who fair-haired young scullion is.'

This was the man who had nearly fallen over the dragon on the first day. He was often about in the kitchens, carrying large pots and platters, and all the heaviest and dirtiest work seemed to be given to him, for he was immensely tall, and strong. Sir Kay was particularly disagreeable to him and seemed to enjoy mocking him.

'Look sharp, now,' he would call out. 'You there with the white hands! Don't dawdle!' And another day: 'Well, Fairhands, how do you like eating with scullions and greasy kitchen boys?'

'I do not like it,' answered the boy proudly, looking at his still white and well-kept hands. 'But I shall bear it, for when twelve months are past I shall be a knight.'

Sir Kay laughed unpleasantly. 'Whoever heard of a kitchen boy being a knight?' he scoffed.

The dragon listened to this with interest and longed to talk with the young scullion whom everyone called Fairhands or Whitehands, or Bewmains, which comes from French and means the same thing.

One morning, Sir Kay tripped over the dragon's tail,

as he was striding angrily into the kitchen. His face went very red, and he kicked the tail as hard as he could. This hurt Sir Kay far more than the dragon, and he limped away, his ears and the back of his neck going a deep purple with fury.

'He won't forgive you,' said a voice, and there was the young man they called Bewmains. 'He'll take it out of you somehow.'

The dragon sighed. He was not enjoying his life in the kitchen. The smell of food, the constant temptation of juicy joints of meat and roasting birds on the spits, the rudeness of the turnspits, and the unkindness of Sir Kay, all made him sigh for Cornwall and his carefree life by the sea, amid the rocks and caves. Once or twice he even planned to run away.

One afternoon, when life had become quite unbearable, he crawled away into a corner of the scullery and put his head under the sink and wept. He found a large spotted handkerchief lying on the draining-board and he borrowed it to weep into.

'Where can I have left it?' he heard a voice ask rather crossly. There was a stamping of feet, and whoever it was came into the scullery. 'Hullo,' said the voice, in a friendly tone, to the dragon's humped back. 'Seen a red spotted handkerchief anywhere?'

The dragon rather reluctantly handed it to him. 'Is this it?' he asked with a snuffle.

'Why, yes, my best one. Where did you find it?'

'On the draining-board.'

'Goodness! It's very wet ... Dragon, Dragon, come here! Come out! I believe you are crying.'

The dragon slowly put his head out from under the sink. Had it been anyone else he would not have done so, but he recognized the voice of Bewmains, and he did not mind his seeing him with red eyes.

'What's the matter?' asked the scullion, squatting beside him and patting his green paw.

'I hate life,' said the dragon.

'This isn't life,' said Bewmains. 'Not this miserable kitchen. This is only an unimportant part of it.'

'It's an awful part,' snuffled the dragon. 'I hate it. I hate everyone – except you.'

'Well, then,' said Bewmains. 'There's one part of it that is not hateful.'

'Why are you so different?' asked the dragon.

'I just am,' answered Bewmains, proudly. 'Look, come out into the yard. It's sunny now, and warm, and we're off duty for another hour. I'll tell you how I came to the kitchens and you can tell me why you are here – for I'm sure you are too noble a dragon to belong to a kitchen naturally – and that will pass the time away and cheer you up.'

He held out his hand, a strong, clean white hand very different from the greasy palms of the kitchen boys. The dragon took it gratefully and hand in paw they went out through the empty kitchens into the yard. They settled down against the whitewashed wall in the sun, their legs stretched out before them, and some sacking spread out beneath them to cushion them against the flagstones. Bewmains produced a little bag of broken biscuits and put it between them.

'You tell me first who you are,' said the dragon, taking some bits of biscuit out of the bag and feeling much better already.

'I cannot reveal my name or my family,' said Bewmains. 'No one must know that until I have proved myself a true knight and been knighted by Sir Lancelot. But I will tell you one thing – I am not what I seem.'

'I thought not,' said the dragon. 'How did you come here?'

'Every year in the month of May, the King holds a great feast. He will not sit down to this feast until he has heard some strange adventure. I had a mind to join his court, yet I did not want to come there under my own name, which would have been well known to the King. I wanted to win myself a name by my own endeavour. I wanted high adventure. I longed to win my knighthood for my deeds alone and not because of my name, so I rode to the King's castle about the time of the feast, with two squires and my little dwarf, Priddy. I stood before the King and I begged two gifts; one I wanted to have straight away, and the other in twelve months' time.

'"Now, ask," said the King, "and I will grant your requests."

'"Sir," said I, "I ask that you will give me meat and drink for this next twelve months, at the end of which time I will beg my other gift."

'"My fair son," said King Arthur, "you shall have meat and drink, but first, tell me your name?"

'"Sir," said I, "that I cannot do."'

The dragon looked closely at Bewmains. 'And what did he say to that?' he asked.

'The King was astonished that I would not, or could not, tell him my name and he put me in the charge of Sir Kay, the steward, to be given meat and drink for twelve months. Alas, Sir Kay persuaded the King that I was of mean and humble birth, fit only to be a scullion, for, he said, had I been of noble birth, I would have said so, and asked for a horse and armour and a place among his knights.'

Bewmains fell silent.

'Well,' said the dragon at last. 'Why didn't you?'

'I have tried to tell you,' answered Bewmains, at last. 'To test myself. If I am to be a true knight, I did not want it to be too easy. I have courage, and I have strength. I wanted to see if I could endure not merely wounds to my body but to my pride. So I welcomed even the unkindness and insulting behaviour of Sir Kay.'

'Why,' said the dragon, with surprise, 'I have done much the same thing. I could have fought my way out of the castle yard. I could have lived in the woods and fields round about, eating people's flocks, and being a bold, bad dragon, but that is just what they wanted to think of me, the King and his court, after they had heard of the King's dream. So I thought I would show them how wrong they were. I would be gentle and peace-loving. When the twelve months is over, I too shall ask a gift of the King and it will be that I may go on a quest.'

'What sort of quest?' asked Bewmains, deeply interested. But at that moment they heard the stamping of feet and the harsh voice of Sir Kay, ordering the boys back to work. 'I shall have to go,' whispered Bewmains. 'Tell me tomorrow.'

Sir Kay appeared in the open doorway. 'Come, come, Whitehands!' he cried. 'No time for sitting in the sun and talking to that idle good-for-nothing beast. In with you, and scour the pans that were burnt this morning.' It was Sir Kay's habit to give Bewmains the dirtiest and most unpleasant jobs he could find.

The dragon followed Sir Kay back into the kitchen, where the King's steward paused to scold the cook for the lack of spice in the gingerbread. 'If I taste gingerbread like that again,' he shouted, 'I'll put the ginger into you myself, my man . . . with the end of my stick!'

The dragon blew out an immense ring of green smoke which settled over the head of Sir Kay like a horse collar.

The cook began to giggle behind his hand and one of the turnspits uttered a guffaw. Sir Kay, bewildered, put up a hand to brush away the offending smoke which swirled round him. It went up his nose, and he began to sneeze. For a moment, he glared at the cook and the turnspits, but it is difficult to be dignified when your nose is full of smoke and your eyes are beginning to stream. Sneezing and wiping his hand across his eyes, he stamped out of the kitchen. When he had gone, the dragon walked softly into the scullery where Bewmains was scouring the pans.

'They are horrible,' groaned the young man. 'Burnt black. I shall never get them clean. A curse on these lazy cooks for letting the porridge burn this morning.'

'The tip of my tail,' said the dragon, 'is as rough as sandpaper. It gets rough dragging on the ground, you see,' he explained. 'I'm not like that all over, of course.'

'I'm sure you are not,' said Bewmains, smoothing a polished yellow fin.

'Well,' said the dragon, 'let's see if my tail-tip gets it clean.'

Bewmains held the pan and the dragon whisked his tail-tip vigorously round and round inside. In a few moments it was shining as bright as a mirror.

'Thank you,' said Bewmains gratefully. 'I'll show it to Sir Kay.'

CHAPTER SIX

The Giant Cook

NEXT day, the dragon was snoozing under the long
kitchen table. This was, he had found, a good place for
getting out of the way, for it was very long; in fact just
about as long as he was when stretched full length. Under
it he was not likely to be tripped over or trodden on, or
have boiling soup spilt on him. Here he was, then, the
following morning, while the kitchens were buzzing
with work. There was a smell of roasting meat, a sound of
sizzling, and bursts of talk and laughter from the scullions
and turnspits. Suddenly he heard Sir Kay's voice. It was a
loud, harsh voice, and cut through all the noise of the
kitchens like the rasp of a saw. The dragon shut his eyes
tightly and put his paws over his ears. He hated Sir Kay.
He could still hear the muffled words, however.

'Now, young man,' Sir Kay was saying. 'Here's the

kitchen. You'll work under the orders of the head cook. His name's Grillo. Obey *his* orders and *my* orders and no one else's. You understand? If you don't cook properly, you'll be sent down among the scullions, and if you can't clean pots and pans, you may end up as a turnspit. It's up to you. Do your work well and you'll get sixpence a year in wages and all your meals thrown in free, and a straw pallet in the stable. What more can you want, eh?'

'Nothing, Your Honour, indeed to goodness,' said a sing-song voice.

Then the dragon heard Sir Kay's heavy feet stamping out of the kitchen. He opened one eye and saw, walking past the table, a pair of legs that he recognized. He reached out and dug a claw gently into the soft leather shoe. The feet stopped, and Bewmain's face bent down to him.

'You bad dragon!' he said crossly. 'You might have made me drop the whole basket.' He was carrying a great brown wicker basket of loaves on his shoulder. 'What is it, anyway?' he asked, setting the loaves down on the floor.

The dragon took one and ate it, absent-mindedly. 'Who is the new cook?' he asked. 'I heard Sir Kay ordering him about.'

'The new cook?' whispered Bewmains. 'Oh, Dragon, only wait till you see him! He'll give you such a surprise!'

'Why?' asked the dragon, with interest. 'Has he only one eye, or two heads, or a pair of horns, like those monsters I used to see sometimes, swimming round the coast of Cornwall? *They* don't surprise me any more. I'm used to monsters.'

'No, no,' said Bewmains. 'He's got the usual number of eyes, but he's a *giant*. He's huge. He's twice as tall as I am. Look, there are his feet.'

Bewmains pointed, and walking past the table went an enormous pair of bare feet – stump! stump! stump!

'Oh!' the dragon's eyes grew round. 'My!' he exclaimed. 'He'll take some feeding.'

Bewmains laughed, gave him a friendly pat, picked up his basket of bread and went off. The large feet had stopped near the dragon. He heard a voice, a slow, almost foreign voice, say: 'Cut up the meat, is it? Aye, give us the chopper, and I'll cut it up, whateffer.'

There was a sound of heavy chopping on the table above the dragon's head. He reached out a paw and ran his claws lightly over the huge, bare foot. The chopping ceased. The new cook stamped his foot, rubbed it up the calf of his other leg, and then went on chopping. After a few minutes, the dragon tried again. This time he pressed a claw rather firmly into the new cook's right ankle. There was a bellow of 'Ow! Something's biting me!' and a great hand reached down and scratched the ankle, followed by a red face, peering anxiously to see what had bitten him.

'Welcome to our kitchen,' said the dragon, politely.

The face disappeared quickly, and the dragon heard an exclamation of: 'Whateffer is it? Is it a sea-serpent?'

The face reappeared, round-eyed.

'How do you do?' asked the dragon.

'Oh, my goodness!' said the face. 'What a beautiful creature you are! All green and gold, is it? I never saw such a sight. Indeed, you are as beautiful as a dream!'

'I am actually a dragon,' said the creature, modestly, turning a front paw over and inspecting his claws thoughtfully.

'To think of it!' cried the voice. 'A dragon! Oh, the good fortune of it – to be a cook in a king's kitchen, with a dragon!'

At that point there was a roar of: 'Cook, get on with your work!' The face disappeared and the feet with it.

The dragon grew thoughtful. He propped his chin on one green paw, and closed his eyes. 'I wonder,' he said to himself. 'There *is* a likeness. The hair is red for one thing. But why should he be here – as a cook? No, no. I don't suppose there is anything in it. One must not jump to conclusions. After all, giants are not uncommon. Many of them must have red hair. It's all too unlikely. All the same, I must get him to tell me about himself. Being a giant, he may know other giants. He might have met the lost son of Jubeance and Martha – who knows?'

The dragon did not have another chance to observe the new cook for several days, and then it was because of a terrible to-do in the kitchens. Sir Kay came striding in during the morning, his brow as black as thunder.

'Who cooked the bacon for breakfast?' he demanded.

The head cook, Grillo, looked frightened.

'I did, Your Honour,' he said, his knees knocking together.

'Uneatable!' roared Sir Kay. 'Had to throw it out of the window. Tasted of something extraordinary. Mustn't happen again.'

'I'll look into the matter at once,' said the head cook. 'I'm very sorry, Your Honour. You know I always cook the breakfast bacon myself to make sure it's exactly to His Majesty's liking, for I always say it's best to start the day well, with a good breakfast. Puts people in a good temper.'

'I am not in a good temper,' said Sir Kay, 'and nor is anyone else. You'd better get dinner served early.'

'Yes, Your Honour,' muttered Grillo.

As soon as Sir Kay had gone, the cook became quite a different man. He shouted for all the undercooks, lined them up in a row and said angrily: 'The breakfast was uneatable, and I – I, Grillo, the head cook of King Arthur's court, am blamed for it. One of you must be responsible and I shall dismiss him as an example to you all. Who fetched the cooking fat this morning and put it in the pan for me?'

An unfortunate young cook stepped forward.

'Ah,' said Grillo, sternly. 'William, was it? Very well, William, you are dismissed. Join the scullions!'

The wretched William departed weeping, and the cook set his underlings to work as fast as they could to get the dinner ready.

However, only three days later Sir Kay came storming into the kitchen again. This time he lined all the cooks up himself.

'Which of you,' he shouted, 'which of you miserable saucepan-stirrers, you unworthy pot-boilers, was responsible for the marchpane served at supper last night?'

One of the cooks stepped forward. He was a big burly fellow called Peter Pastry, and he did not show the slightest fear. 'It was the finest marchpane I've ever made,' he said stubbornly, folding his huge arms and glaring at Sir Kay.

'You're dismissed!' roared Sir Kay.

'I'm dismissed, am I?' said Peter Pastry, calmly, 'No one else can make marchpane shapes as I can, or pastry figures of animals, or jellies like castles or blancmanges with domes like a church. If you don't want me, I know who does. I'll to France and work for the French King. They appreciate a good pastry cook in France.'

And with that he walked out of the kitchen and was never seen again. Sir Kay was very put out, even more over losing such a good cook as Peter Pastry than over the nasty taste of the marchpane.

'What happened to those who ate it?' asked the new cook, who was called David, innocently.

'They were seized with violent stomach-ache,' answered Sir Kay. 'Many of them lay down and rolled in agony among the rushes.'

'Have any died?' asked David.

Sir Kay looked sharply at him. 'No,' he said. 'What do you know about it, young man?'

'Nothing,' said the giant cook, looking down at his large feet.

There was no more trouble for a week or two. Then it started again. Something tasted odd, knights were taken ill, cooks were dismissed, or food turned bad. But it was never discovered who was at the bottom of it. It was all very mysterious.

The dragon went on wondering about the giant cook. Sometimes he thought he had King Jubeance's nose. Another time, he thought he saw a resemblance in the chin to Queen Martha, but it seemed so unlikely that the young son of a giant king should have ended up as a cook in the kitchens of King Arthur that he didn't very seriously consider it. He was still determined, when his year was up, to beg the King for his boon, which was to have the right to go on a quest in search of the missing Giles.

Meanwhile the days passed slowly by. There were friendly conversations with Bewmains, and amusing tricks from the new cook, who would keep all the kitchen servants in fits of laughter of an evening, when the work was done. He could make things disappear, toss a ball to the ceiling and make it stick there till he told it to come down. He could produce a white mouse out of a scullion's ear, or make one of the roasting turkeys cry Cock-a-doodle-doo! He was a very clever, good-humoured young man. Altogether, though the dragon had days of boredom and even unhappiness, he was surprised to find how time was passing.

Soon after the dragon had come to the kitchens, he had drawn a calendar on the whitewashed wall in a dark corner where no one ever looked. It was a long row of rather crooked squares, three hundred and sixty-five of

them, one for each day of the year. Every night, before he
went to sleep on his hard bed under the kitchen table, he
used to take a little piece of charred wood from the fire
and fill in a square. Nearly half of them were blacked in
now. He felt more cheerful when he looked at them.

One cold clear night in January, when the stars were
brilliant although there was no moon, the dragon went
out for a breath of air, for the kitchens became unbearably
stuffy by evening. Someone was in the courtyard, and
whoever it was slunk quickly away out of sight down a
dark passage. The dragon was curious. He thought it
might be a robber, and to kill or capture a robber might
win him good words from his enemy, Sir Kay, and make
his time in the kitchens pleasanter. So he crossed the yard,
and as he nosed along the wall, he suddenly noticed, so
bright was the starlight, some squares very like his own,
rows and rows of them, all very straight and tidy. More

than half were filled in. The dragon paused and looked closely at them.

'Odd!' he said to himself. 'Someone else is doing it, too.'

Then he remembered the robber and crept quietly towards the dark passage on the other side of the yard. 'I will smoke him out,' he thought, so he blew a puff of smoke through the narrow doorway. Nothing happened. He went warily a little way into the entrance and blew as much smoke as he could. A choking cough came from the far end.

'Aha!' cried the dragon. 'I have you! Surrender or die!'

'Stop it, Dragon!' came a voice he knew. 'You're half killing me. I didn't know who it was coming out into the yard. I thought it must be Sir Kay.' Bewmains groped his way out of the passage with his sleeve held over his mouth and his eyes streaming. 'Silly old dragon,' he said affectionately. 'If you must choke anyone, choke Sir Kay.'

The dragon pointed to the squares on the wall. 'Did you do those?' he asked.

'Of course I did,' said Bewmains. 'It helps to make the time pass quickly.'

'I do it too,' said the dragon. 'Mine's on a wall in the kitchen.'

'Three hundred and sixty-five days in these horrible kitchens,' groaned Bewmains, 'and oh, how I long for them to be over, so that I can go on my quest and win my knighthood.'

'So do I,' agreed the dragon.

'You've never told me about your quest,' said Bewmains. 'Tell me about it now.'

'All right, but it's getting cold,' answered the dragon. 'Let's go in and sit under the table for a bit and I'll tell you.'

The kitchen was in darkness. Only a faint glow of red embers showed in the dying fire. Occasionally a small flame flickered up, and then its reflection winked from the shining copper pans which stood along the dressers. From the corners came the heavy breathing and occasional snores of the turnspits and potboys and scullions as they slept on bundles of straw. The dragon and Bewmains sat quietly under the table, and the dragon whispered to his friend the story of Giant Jubeance and Martha and the kidnapping of their only son, Giles. 'And when the year is over,' ended the dragon, seriously, 'the King will give me the gift he promised me.'

'And what will you do?' asked Bewmains.

'I shall set out on my quest to find the long-lost son of Jubeance and Martha,' said the dragon.

'Alone?' asked Bewmains.

'No. I shall ask Gryfflet to come with me. Dear Gryfflet,' said the dragon and sighed. 'He is foolish and not very brave, but he is good. He has a true heart. I wouldn't want anyone else – except you, of course, and I can't have you, I suppose?'

'No,' said Bewmains, gazing into the almost dead fire. 'No, Dragon, I don't think you can have me. I shall have a quest too, though I do not know yet what it will be, but quests must be made alone, except for one's squire, or servant. We are both seeking knighthood. We can't do it together.'

'Perhaps,' said the dragon hopefully, gripping Bewmains' hand, 'perhaps our paths may cross sometimes?'

'Perhaps they may,' said Bewmains. 'I hope they do.'

He yawned. 'I'm sleepy. I must go to bed. Good night, Dragon.'

And with that, he tiptoed across the kitchen, for he slept with the other kitchen boys on the dirty, cold floor, with only a piece of sacking for a blanket. The dragon laid his head down on his paws, and dreamed of his quest and his triumphant return with Giles, and the joy of Jubeance and Martha when they saw their long-lost son again.

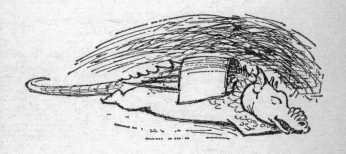

CHAPTER SEVEN

The Quest of Bewmains

MEANWHILE, as most of the undercooks had been dismissed, David, the giant, had become quite an important person, and so good-natured was he and so full of laughs that everyone liked him. He was well known for his tricks now and some of the knights would even put their heads in at the kitchen door, sometimes, to watch him. His practical jokes and conjuring tricks amused the kitchen endlessly in the long evenings. He made live rabbits pop up out of the cauldron, and once a whole chorus of pigeons pushed their heads through the crust of a pigeon pie and cooed melodiously. Everyone was delighted.

So the time passed, and soon Bewmains would be leaving the kitchens. This plunged the dragon into the deepest gloom. He used even to weep a little to himself at night, under the table, when he thought of what life would be like without the kindly, generous Bewmains. He liked the giant cook well enough but there was something odd about him. He was so unexpected, always up to some curious trick; and his whole life seemed wrapped in mystery. Sometimes he looked scared, and would speak to no one, but crept round the kitchen looking anxiously over his shoulder as though he expected to see someone he feared. At other times he was as gay as a lark. Once the dragon tried to question him. 'Where do you come from?' he asked.

'I don't know,' replied the giant, and suddenly that scared look came over his face. 'I just know I was brought up in Wales. I never learned the name of the place.'

'How odd,' observed the dragon. 'And your name – I suppose you've got another name?'

'Oh no,' answered the giant. 'I'm just David. At least, I believe I had another name, but *she* wouldn't tell me what it was. She said I'd tell it to people and then I'd be taken away from her.'

'Odder still,' said the dragon, frowning. 'And who is *she*?'

'She's the grand lady who brought me up. Aunt Mor, I called her,' said the giant. 'She's beautiful – sometimes – though she can look horrible too. She's very clever. She taught me all I know. If only I'd been cleverer,' he sighed, 'I could have learned so much more, but I'm a stupid fellow.' He banged his head with his fist. 'I believe my head's made of wood,' he said, ruefully.

'And what was her proper name?' asked the dragon. 'I suppose you never knew that either?'

The giant looked hard at the dragon. 'No,' he said. 'She was just Aunt Mor.'

'This is a useless conversation,' said the dragon, rather annoyed. 'To know neither one's name, nor one's home, nor one's aunt's name – it's just careless and ignorant.'

The giant looked huffy. 'Well, she taught me a lot, anyway,' he said. 'I bet you can't do this.' He waved an enormous fist in the air and opened it under the dragon's nose. On it sat a white mouse.

'I am not interested in mice, white or otherwise,' said the dragon, and walked stiffly away. But he did not stop thinking. 'I wonder,' he said to himself. 'It could be,' he said an hour later. 'I'm not sure it isn't,' he said, the next morning.

There was now only one day before Bewmains was due to leave the kitchens for good, and claim his gifts from the King. It was the time of the annual May feast and great were the preparations for it. In the afternoon Sir Kay told the kitchen boys and scullions and turnspits and cooks that they were all to go up to the royal wardrobe-master where they would be given new clothes to wear on the feast day. The only one who didn't go was David, the giant cook. Being so large, there was nothing to fit him in the Camelot wardrobe. His new tunic was being specially made for him and would be ready that night.

So it was that he was alone in the kitchen that afternoon. The dragon was snoozing in the sun in the courtyard outside. Every now and then he would hear David chuckling to himself, as he performed some ridiculous trick for his own amusement, but the dragon was too warm and comfortable to bother to go in and watch him. Suddenly he heard another voice, a sharp female voice. He pricked up his ears.

'So this is what I find!' said the voice. 'I thought as much! Nearly a year has gone by and you have done nothing. Here are all the preparations for the feast, for the feast of the year, you idle villain, and no one about, to see what poisons you put into the dishes, and all you can do is sit pulling white mice out of your sleeves and turning eggs into dumplings. Take that!' There was the sound of a slap. 'Oh, you lazy, good-for-nothing boy! Is it for this I brought you up in Wales all those years? Is it for this I taught you my magic arts? What were my instructions? (slap!) Come on, you wretch, tell me! (slap!) What were my orders when I secured you a post as cook in the King's kitchens?'

'P-please,' came the tearful voice of David. 'P-please, I was to p-p-p-poison the King.'

'Exactly,' came the rasping voice. 'Ex-actly. And what have you done? Have you so much as poisoned a rat?'

'I did try, Aunt Mor, really I did try.'

'Try, indeed!'

'They fell sick, two or three times they did, Aunt Mor.'

'What was the good of that, you fool? It didn't KILL anybody.'

'The magic wasn't strong enough, Aunt. You should have taught me a different kind.'

'Different kind indeed!' the voice rose to a shriek. 'I taught you all I needed to teach you. Why should I give away my secrets, you worthless wretch? You had strength enough to make my magic work, and you've done nothing, nothing. You're coming back with me now,' the voice continued. 'I'm not leaving you in this kitchen wasting time and magic on silly tricks, and poisoning nobody. My coach is outside. We'll drive to Wales to-night, and then – we'll see!'

The dragon could hear the footsteps of the woman and the unhappy cook leaving the kitchen. He ran to the wall of the courtyard. By standing on his back legs and stretching his neck, he could just see over the top of the wall. There, driving away, was an enormous coach with the giant's head and shoulders sticking out of it. The dragon waved, and the giant waved back with a despairing cry. Just before it disappeared, the dragon saw, with his sharp eyes, the doors of the coach, and the painted coat of arms upon them. It was moving away too fast for him to see clearly, but it looked as if there were three black cooking-pots on the shield. Three black cooking-pots . . .

The dragon was immensely excited. What could it mean, except that David, the giant cook, was none other than Giles? Somehow, somewhere, there was a connection between the woman who had kidnapped him, and Aunt Mor who knew King Arthur's court and had secured for him the job as cook. *Who was Aunt Mor?* The dragon had not seen her, but her voice sounded old, and cracked and ugly. She sounded like a witch. The dragon thought back over the story of the kidnapping. The farm boy and the silly nursemaid had said that the lady in the cooking-pot coach had been *beautiful*. The dragon was puzzled. Could a beautiful lady have a harsh, witch-like voice like the one he had just heard?

I suppose it is possible, he thought.

That night, Bewmains' last night in the kitchens, the dragon told him of his discovery. 'Oh, if only I were going to be free tomorrow,' groaned the dragon. 'Every day will make it more difficult to find him.' And he almost wept with vexation.

Bewmains put a hand on his paw. 'Listen, Dragon,' he said, 'if the King is in a good mood tomorrow, when I ask for my gifts, I will plead with him to release you.'

The dragon gazed at him.

'Bewmains,' he said, 'you are a true friend.'

'I can't promise anything, of course,' went on the young man. 'But you have been a model dragon, and I don't see why he shouldn't grant me my wish, if I plead for you.'

The dragon could hardly wait till the next day. The coach was getting farther and farther away every moment and the only clues he had were a shield with cooking-pots on it and a harsh voice which had said, 'We're going to Wales.' It wasn't very much on which to begin a quest.

The next morning, Bewmains said good-bye to the kitchen boys and the scullions and the cooks. He said a special farewell to the dragon, who was hiding under the table.

'Cheer up, old Dragon!' he whispered. 'I'll do my very best for you. In any case, we are sure to meet again one day. Dragons never despair!'

The dragon shook hands silently and with a heavy heart watched his friend leave the kitchen. Soon Bewmains reached the great hall of Camelot, which was hung with banners for the feast. Here were gathered all the knights and the King himself, waiting for the strange adventure without which the King would not allow the feast to begin. It was very late in the morning when a squire came hurrying into the hall, and kneeling before the King, said: 'Sire, you may begin the feast. Here comes a damsel with a strange adventure to tell.'

Then the King was glad. He sat down, and all the

knights with him, and they began to eat and drink while they listened to what the damsel had to say.

'Sir,' she began, 'I have a sister, and she is besieged in her castle by a wicked knight, so that she cannot get out. I have come to you for help because here are gathered the noblest knights in the world.'

'What is your sister called?' asked the King, 'and where is her castle? What is the name of the knight who besieges her?'

'O King,' replied the damsel, 'I may not tell you my sister's name, but the name of the wicked knight is the Red Knight of the Red Lands, and the name of the castle is Castle Perilous, which stands on the River Usk, on the borders of Wales and your own fair kingdom.'

Now the King was not pleased that she refused to give her sister's name. He did not wish to send out one of his valiant knights on a quest which was so uncertain, and for this reason he denied her request unless she would tell her sister's name.

'I will seek elsewhere,' said the damsel, proudly.

But Bewmains leapt to his feet and stood before the King. 'Sir King, I have been this twelvemonth in your kitchens and now I claim my gift.'

'Ask then, upon my peril,' said the King.

'Sir, this shall be my request: that you will grant me this adventure, to ride to the help of this damsel's sister.'

'You shall have it,' said the King, after a moment's reflection.

The damsel was very angry when she heard the King's words. 'What!' she cried. 'Shall I have a man who has been your kitchen boy!' And she left the hall, mounted her horse and rode away.

With that, Bewmains began to arm himself with all

speed, and his armour was brought to him by a dwarf, no one knew how or why. But you who are reading this chronicle will remember that Bewmains first came to Camelot with a dwarf in attendance upon him. The armour lacked a spear and a shield, but it was of fine workmanship and there were many who said to each other, 'This can be no common kitchen boy. He wears his armour like one who is nobly born.'

Then Bewmains said farewell to the King, and to Gawaine and Lancelot, and before he went, he knelt before Arthur and said in a low voice: 'I have no right to ask another gift, Sir King, but it is not for myself that I ask it.'

'What is it?' asked Arthur.

'In your kitchens lies a noble dragon. His year there

will end in a month's time, but he longs for his freedom and he has an important quest to pursue that will not wait. Will you set him free?'

Arthur thought for a moment. Then Guinevere leaned across the table and said: 'Remember, he is the dragon from Cornwall.'

'I will free him,' said the King.

While Bewmains was setting forth in his glorious armour, with a saddle-cloth of gold, and his dwarf beside him, Sir Gryfflet was on his way to the kitchen to tell the dragon that the King had set him free a month before his time there was ended. He found the dragon lying under the long table on the dirty, greasy floor. Cooks were chopping up meat just above his head, and scullions were tramping backwards and forwards with piles of dishes and

platters. Turnspits stood by the fire, winding the handles of the sizzling spits, shouting to each other and laughing and singing. The noise and confusion had driven the dragon to take refuge under the table, but as soon as he heard Sir Grvfflet's voice, he leapt up, forgetting the great kitchen table above him. He ran towards his old friend, with the table tipped up on his back, leaving the astonished cooks standing with their meat-knives in their hands while the turnspits stopped their noise to gape and stare. The dragon shook Gryfflet warmly by both hands, and, feeling something on his back, shrugged his shoulders. The huge table fell to the floor with a crash, upside down.

The dragon glanced behind him. 'Never mind,' he said heartlessly. 'They have trodden on my tail often enough. Gryfflet, am I to be freed?'

'You are free,' replied the knight. 'Come to the great hall. You have a gift to ask from the King.'

'One minute,' said the dragon. He quickly hurried over to the wall by the fire, picked up a charred piece of wood and scrabbled on the wall with it. 'My calendar,' he explained. 'How wonderful to be able to scratch off the whole month as though it were one day.'

Sir Gryfflet begged the dragon to come away, but he said there was one more thing he must do, and standing firmly in the middle of the disordered kitchen he cried out in his loudest voice: 'Cooks, scullions and turnspits! For nearly a year, I have dwelt in your midst. From you I have endured hard words, laughter and unfeeling jokes. Now that I am leaving you, I give you a piece of advice. I happen to be a dragon of noble descent. I consider it beneath my dignity to bite kitchen boys and turnspits. I would scorn to eat a cook. But other dragons are not so noble-minded as I am. Beware of dragons, my friends.

One day you may meet with one who has no scruples about eating you up if you annoy him.'

It was a dreadful and necessary warning which they would have done well to heed. Little more than a year later, a frightful dragon, very different from the gentle Cornish beast, came into Arthur's kingdom, savaging and slaughtering. The King and his knights were away in Scotland, and this monster made his way into the kitchens at Camelot, and ate everyone, down to the last scullion and the smallest turnspit.

Having made this solemn and awe-inspiring speech, the dragon hurried with Sir Gryfflet to the great hall of the castle of Camelot, and bowed low before the King, 'Your Majesty,' he said, with dignity. 'I have served for eleven months in your kitchens, and despite many insults and hard words, I have not bitten a single scullion's leg, nor chewed a single turnspit's toe. Nor have I eaten one morsel of meat. Now that you have released me, I ask you to give me the gift you promised.'

'What is it?' asked the King.

'I desire to go on a quest.'

Sir Kay and one or two other knights laughed scornfully at this. The dragon turned upon them an angry yellow eye and blew a small puff of green smoke from his jaws. 'Perhaps you forget,' he said, sternly, 'that I am free now.'

The knights fell silent. The Queen then leaned forward. 'Noble Dragon,' she said, 'what is this quest?'

'I go to seek one who is lost. He is the son of good people whom I met on my travels. He was stolen when a child and I believe I know where he is. I shall quest until I find him.'

The dragon did not say that the lost child might be

the giant cook who had served in the kitchens. He knew that it is always best to keep things to yourself as far as possible.

The King was puzzled at the dragon's words. 'It is a worthy quest,' he said at length, 'and I will grant you your wish. But you must have an escort and I will send with you your old friend, Sir Gryfflet, armed and mounted. Is there anything else you need?'

'I would like to take Starlight, as well,' said the dragon.

So the King gave orders that Starlight was to be loaded with provisions for the journey: a large sack of oatmeal for porridge, a sack of apples, several whole cheddar cheeses, a bag of sugar and a bag of walnuts.

'That should last us for a week or so,' observed the dragon, as he checked over the amounts.

Gryfflet sighed. He did not care much for this vegetarian diet, and wished he could have taken along a side of beef.

'No,' said the dragon, firmly. 'It is good for one to give up things. It strengthens the will. You will be a better knight, as I am a better dragon, for having given up meat and taken to porridge.'

'But you *like* porridge and I don't,' groaned Sir Gryfflet.

'That is quite beside the point,' said the dragon.

CHAPTER EIGHT

The Dragon's Quest Begins

THEY set out from Camelot, on a fine summer morning,
the dragon snuffing the fresh air with enjoyment. They
had travelled for some miles in silence, when suddenly
they heard the sound of horses' hooves upon the road
behind them. They turned and saw Sir Kay, galloping
towards them as fast as he could, his horse all in a lather.
He reined up with a jerk, and looked at the two of them
very disagreeably.

'Have you seen the kitchen boy, Bewmains?' he
demanded.

The dragon scratched one ear and thought for some
time in silence, while Sir Kay tapped his foot impatiently
against his horse's flank. At last the dragon said: 'I might
have, and yet again I mightn't.'

'You two were as thick as thieves,' barked Sir Kay.
'I thought he might have waited for you.'

'I do not care for the expression "as thick as thieves",' said the dragon, eyeing Sir Kay's stout leg.

Sir Kay backed his horse away hastily. 'Well, you have *not* seen him then?' he said, rather more politely.

'I didn't say one thing or the other,' answered the dragon, sitting down by the roadside, and examining his paws. 'I believe I have a blister, already,' he said. 'Gryffiet, did you bring any sticking plaster?'

'Will you answer me?' roared Sir Kay.

'No, I will not!' roared back the dragon, so angrily that Sir Kay's horse reared on its hind legs and bolted with him. 'Aha!' said the dragon. 'Things are different now.'

'I hope he doesn't find Bewmains,' said Sir Gryfflet, anxiously. 'He will be in a terrible temper. He might harm him.'

'Harm Bewmains?' The dragon smiled. 'He is more than a match for that ruffian, Sir Kay.'

'Is he?' went on Sir Gryfflet, seriously. 'There was an odd thing about Bewmains. I don't believe you knew of it. His dwarf brought him the most beautiful armour, and a saddle-cloth of gold for his horse. I saw it myself. But he brought him no spear and no shield. Nothing but a sword.'

The dragon pricked up his ears. 'Only a sword?' he repeated. 'In that case, yes, we *will* hurry. He may be in some danger, for Sir Kay was heavily armed.'

He set off at a brisk pace, with Gryfflet riding beside him at a trot, leading the laden Starlight. Ahead of them in the distance the road began to climb over high hills, and they could just see Sir Kay, a tiny black dot, disappearing as it went over the top.

'We shall never catch them up,' panted Sir Gryfflet.

'I don't believe we shall,' agreed the dragon, stopping and sitting down in the road. 'But I could fly, couldn't I?'

'What about me?' asked the knight.

'You could just plod on on horseback.'

'But how shall I know where you are?' wailed Sir Grydflet. 'I'll never find you again in those hills. You might fly anywhere.'

The dragon scanned the horizon. On the bare, distant hills could be seen a clump of trees, a good landmark.

'Make for that,' said the dragon, pointing, 'and I'll meet you there – the day after tomorrow. If I am not there, wait for me. I'll come, never fear.'

Then he stretched out his wings and took off in the direction of the hills. These hills, which are called the Mendips, are high and bleak, and dotted with pits called swallet-holes. In the hills dwell dwarfish men who dig for a metal called lead. Bewmains' dwarf, Priddy, was one of these very miners, and it was well that Bewmains had him as a guide, for he knew the country like the back of his hand. He stayed with Bewmains and his lady throughout the whole quest. When the young man had travelled a year ago from the Orkneys, right through Scotland and England to Camelot, he had ridden through these same Mendip hills and had made friends with the dwarf miners. Priddy, who was an armourer, had made for the Scotsman the splendid armour he wore when he set out on his quest, while the sword was also designed by him and was the finest he had ever forged.

The dragon looked down as he flew and saw the Mendip hills rising beneath him. He began to glide downwards, searching everywhere for a glimpse of armour. Suddenly he saw a flash of steel, and as he circled lower he could hear clashes and shouts. Two knights were struggling in mortal combat, one armed with spear and shield, the other with nothing but a sword. The dragon blew out a huge puff of green smoke. The two men paused and looked up and one of them cried, 'Ho, Dragon!' at which the dragon shouted back, 'Ho, Bewmains!'

Then the two knights went for each other again. Bewmains, sword in hand, rushed at Sir Kay and with a mighty stroke knocked his spear out of his hand. It rose into the air and the dragon caught it in one paw. In a moment, Bewmains had thrust his sword into Sir Kay's side, and the knight lay bleeding on the ground. The dwarf ran up and seized Sir Kay's shield.

'Here, master!' he cried. 'Here is the shield you needed.'

'And here,' said the dragon, alighting upon the ground close at hand, 'is a spear for you.'

Sir Kay groaned. He was too hurt to say insulting words any more. Bewmains went over to him and tied a piece of linen round his wound. 'Help him to his horse,' he told the dwarf. 'He is not seriously hurt and can easily ride back to Camelot. He should have known better than to ride after me and try to kill me.'

So Sir Kay was heaved on to his charger. The dwarf turned the horse's head towards Camelot, and Sir Kay jolted off down the road, groaning and muttering.

Bewmains turned to the dragon. 'It is good to see you free,' he said, 'and I should like to talk with you, but I cannot wait. My damsel, the Lady Lynette, is already far ahead of me, and I must hasten to overtake her, for I am riding to the rescue of her sister.'

'And I am searching for the lost David,' said the dragon. 'My quest has begun. I am on my way to Wales.'

'Go and see my brother dwarfs in Ubley Warren, over the hill yonder,' called the dwarf. 'Priddy is my

name. They all know me. Tell them Priddy sent you and they will help you if they can. Your lost David may have passed through the Mendips on his way to Wales.'

With that, Bewmains and his dwarf hastened on, to catch up with the damsel. The dragon knew that it would be some hours before Gryfflet reached the hills so he made his way in the direction the dwarf had pointed out. It was then that he suddenly remembered Starlight – Starlight on whose back was the sack of oatmeal, and the apples, and cheese and walnuts. Immediately, the dragon felt ravenously hungry. And he had not even a sandwich. How far was it to Ubley Warren? he wondered. One mile, two miles, three miles? He had no idea.

It began to grow dark. He could see the path clearly enough but a mist came down over the hills and blotted out the view. The grass grew wet and dewy, and the dragon's scales and fins grew wet too, as though he were hung with beads of rain. He felt tired and dispirited, and he was worried about Gryfflet. Suppose they never met again at all? An awful thought. And Gryfflet had the food. Suddenly the dragon saw a figure coming towards him. It was an old, bent man, carrying a huge bundle of firewood on his back.

'Good sir,' began the dragon.

'Eh?' wheezed the old man, and peered at him. 'Who are you?' he croaked. 'Don't know your face.'

'I'm a dragon,' said the dragon loudly.

'Never heard of him,' replied the ancient. 'He doesn't live hereabouts.'

'I'm hungry. I want food.'

'I can't say, I'm sure,' said the old man and started to walk on.

'Food!' shouted the dragon. 'Something to eat!'

'No, I can't eat meat,' mumbled the old one. 'Got no teeth now.' He pointed to toothless gums.

'The dragon gave up. 'Ubley?' he queried in quite a soft voice, into the old man's ear. Pointing and questioning, he repeated: 'Ubley Warren?'

This time the ancient heard him clearly. '*Ubley*, d'you want?' he replied. 'Why didn't you say so? Oh, they're a nasty lot. You don't want to go there. You should keep away from them dwarfs.'

The dragon kept his temper with difficulty and said: 'But I *do* want to go there.'

'Well, it's five miles at least,' said the old man. 'Up hill and down dale, through the river, and – oh, I shouldn't go there if I were you. Follow this track, and turn right at the twisted thorn. You'll see the path. But I wouldn't go near 'em myself. A nasty lot, them dwarves.' Mumbling and muttering, he went on his way.

The dragon groaned and plodded on again. His feet were tired and his tail felt as though it were made of lead. It was the first day of his quest and he wished heartily that he were back in the warm kitchen, lying under the table. Even those dry crusts would taste good now, he thought miserably. Then suddenly, ahead of him, a little to the right of the track, he saw a light, then more lights. He could see figures dancing and hear music. A black tree loomed up through the darkness. Against the deep blue sky the dragon could see a strange twisted mass of branches.

'The twisted thorn!' he cried. 'It must be Ubley!'

There was the little path, and the dragon hurried eagerly down it and arrived at the outskirts of a village. The cottages were tiny huts, and some seemed half underground, while others were dug out of the sides of mounds and hillocks. In the streets were flaring torches and a crowd of little people. Some were playing tiny fiddles, and others bagpipes. The noise was cheerful and accompanied by a wooden clatter like the sound of castanets. The dragon wondered what it was and then saw that many of the dwarfs wore wooden shoes and these clacked rhythmically in time to the music, as they danced.

Now, you might think that the dwarves (for so they were) would be frightened of a huge creature like a dragon, but they were not. They are the most fearless people in the world, for they are extremely curious, and their curiosity kills their fear. If a dwarf sees a giant, he doesn't scream with terror. He whips out his tape measure and says to himself: 'I'll just swarm up his legs to his shoulder, for I must find out how tall he is. Maybe he is a bigger giant than the one my brother Ebenezer saw, twenty years ago.' So no sooner had some of the dwarfs seen the dragon approaching than several of them rushed out to inspect him. Said the first: 'He has wings!' Said the second: 'I must count his fins.' Said the third: 'I will just measure his tail.'

The dragon was extremely surprised. 'Shall I blow smoke for you?' he asked.

'In a minute,' said the third dwarf, measuring the dragon's tail with a foot-rule which he had taken from his pocket.

'Three – six – nine – twelve – fifteen —' he muttered.

'Would you mind opening your jaws?' asked another dwarf. 'I just want to count your teeth. I am Banwell, chief tooth-counter, and I haven't any dragon teeth in my records yet.'

The dragon opened his mouth very wide, and the dwarf ran his pencil quickly along the teeth – tap, tap, tap – like a boy running his stick along a row of iron railings. Then he scribbled in his notebook, and the dragon closed his jaws with a snap and stamped his right front paw.

'I am delighted to be an object of scientific interest to you,' he said, scowling, 'but now that you have satisfied your curiosity, will you please satisfy my hunger. I am STARVING.'

'Dear me,' said the dwarf called Banwell, shutting up a small black notebook, with a snap. 'Dear me, seventy-three teeth. An odd number. Very strange.'

'My teeth don't need counting,' bellowed the dragon. 'They need food.'

'We'll see about it at once,' said Banwell, obligingly. 'Wookey! Fetch Cheddar!'

The dwarf called Wookey was the one who had measured the dragon's length. He folded up his foot-rule and hurried into the darkness.

'Now,' said Banwell, 'we shall be most interested to see what you eat and how you eat. Please enter our village carefully. You might tread on someone.'

He led the way, and the dragon began to crawl down the narrow street, while the dancers and fiddlers and bag-pipers backed into doorways and down little alleys.

Soon they came – or rather the dragon's head and shoulders came – into an open square. There were important buildings all round it – Institute of Science, was carved over one doorway, Mining Museum over another and Geological Department over a third.

'Suppose you sit here,' suggested Banwell. 'You can fit in if you leave your tail down the street. Ah, here's Cheddar. He's the master cook of our village.'

Cheddar at once took out a large book labelled *Recipes*.

'I am compiling a new cookery book,' he said, 'and I will add a special chapter on Dragon Food and how to cook it. Now what sort of food do you fancy?'

'Anything,' groaned the dragon.

The dwarf solemnly wrote down 'Anything'.

But the dragon suddenly remembered his vow and added hastily: 'Anything except meat.'

'Except meat,' wrote the dwarf. 'Thank you very much.'

'And now could I have some?' said the dragon faintly. 'I am dying of hunger.'

Cheddar considered, tapping his pencil against his teeth. 'There's a new cheese, just come up from the valley,' he said. 'And there are apples from Clevedon – cart-load came up this week – and walnuts from Weston-super-Mare – they seem to grow well by the sea.'

The dragon's mouth was watering so much that he could hardly speak. 'Those are the very foods I like best,' he cried at last, swallowing hard.

'Splendid!' said Cheddar. 'Your dinner will be served in a couple of minutes.'

Dwarfs were now crawling into the square to look at the dragon. They had brown serious faces, bright eyes and sharp inquisitive noses. The dragon was too tired and hungry to care much about them. He lay with his head on his paws, worn out. Punctually in two minutes' time, there was a rumbling sound and a large Cheddar cheese appeared, rolled along one of the streets leading into the square, by several dwarfs. It was followed by a barrow, on which were loaded the apples and walnuts. The dragon fell to and made a large meal, watched by dozens of beady eyes.

'He has eaten fifteen pounds of Cheddar cheese, six

pounds of walnuts and ten pounds of apples,' said one, reading from his little notebook.

'Why do you write down so many things?' asked the dragon.

'It is important to make notes of everything one sees,' said a learned-looking dwarf, from whose pockets peeped a vast number of pens and pencils, so that he had the appearance of a porcupine. 'Otherwise one never knows anything.'

The dragon considered this. 'What do you do with all this knowledge?' went on the dragon.

'Store it up,' said another dwarf. 'You never know when it might come in useful.'

'I store up things,' said the dragon. 'Seaweed and wooden boxes, and shells, and things – at least, I did,' he added sadly, 'when I lived in a cave in Cornwall.'

This kept them all writing busily for several minutes.

Suddenly, the dragon startled them all by saying, 'Do you remember Priddy?'

At once there was great excitement. 'Priddy!' they all exclaimed. 'Our Priddy! Priddy the Master Smith!'

'I know him,' said the dragon, looking down modestly.

At once the dwarfs began to smile and look friendly and cheerful. 'Any friend of Priddy,' they cried, 'is a friend of ours! What can we do for you?'

Now that the dragon's hunger was satisfied, he was not quite sure what they could do for him, till suddenly he remembered poor Grefflet. The dragon felt very bad that he had not thought of him before. 'I started out on my quest with a friend,' he said, 'and I left him following me on horseback and promised to meet him at the clump of trees on the top of the hills. I must go and find him. He is not very brave and he might be frightened.'

'He's not there yet,' said one of the dwarfs.

'Not there?' exclaimed the dragon. 'How do you know?'

'I'd hear him,' remarked the dwarf. 'It's not that far off. I'd hear him quite plainly.'

'I don't understand,' began the dragon, but Banwell motioned him to be silent.

'Quiet! I think he's just arrived!' cried Banwell.

A deep silence fell over the dark village. Every dwarf seemed to be listening intently. You could almost hear them listening, a curiously noiseless sound, like the silence you get when you open the door of a room and don't know whether anyone is in it or not.

Then the dragon heard, quite clearly, these words, in Gryfflet's voice: 'Dragon! Dragon! Do come, Dragon!'

He looked at the listening faces round him. 'Can you hear it?' he demanded.

'We can hear it,' said Banwell. 'We can hear a voice, a cry, but the words are only for you. Can you understand them?'

'I can!' exclaimed the dragon in great excitement. 'They are the words of my friend Gryfflet. I must get to him! I must get to him quickly!'

'Now don't be in a hurry, Dragon,' advised Wookey, laying a tiny, gnarled hand on the dragon's immense paw. 'You must listen in the right way. It isn't just the ears that you must listen with. Now . . .'

In the deep stillness, the dragon closed his eyes, and listened intently. When the words came again, they were accompanied by a kind of picture which floated into his brain, he couldn't say how. He knew – he was certain he was right – that Gryfflet was down in a deep cleft in the hills, and he knew, too, exactly in which direction he would find him, and that he must fly, even though it was pitch dark.

'Well?' said Wookey. 'Do you know now?'

'Yes,' answered the dragon, confidently.

'Then off you go!' said the dwarf. 'Bring your friend back with you. Any friend of Priddy's is a friend of ours!'

CHAPTER NINE

The Rescue

THE dragon beat his wings and soared up into the air.
Below him, he could see for a minute the tiny lights of
Ubley Warren, the dwarf village. Then he turned south-
west over the black hills, flying fast. He could see the
clump of trees where he was to have met Grynfflet the
following morning. It lay, an even blacker pool on the
dark hilltop, but he knew now that Grynfflet was not
there. He flew steadily on. Ahead of him he could see
where the hill ended and the valley began. The rivers
gleamed faintly in the light of the few stars, and he could
now perceive that the hills were split at one point by

what looked like a huge crack. 'That's the gorge where
Grytflet is!' he cried aloud, and began to glide downwards.
A glint of armour told him where the lost knight stood,
and in a few moments, Grytflet was flinging his arm
round the dragon's neck, almost weeping with relief.

'How did you find me?' he asked. 'How did you know
I was here? Oh, Dragon, I'm so glad to see you!'

The dragon paused. 'I don't know exactly how I
knew,' he answered, at last. 'You called me, didn't you,
and I heard you quite plainly, and then I just came. Why
are you here? I told you I'd meet you tomorrow at the
clump of trees.'

'I know,' said the knight. 'I thought I'd get near the
clump by the evening and be ready waiting for you there

tomorrow. But the clump kept disappearing behind a hill, and I lost it over and over again, and then it grew dark and suddenly we found ourselves going down and down, deep into this cleft. And then' – poor Gryfflet looked very ashamed of himself – 'then I was so frightened that I called out "Dragon! Dragon!" several times, in the hope you'd hear me. My voice echoed back from the rocks in the most horrible manner, as though someone were laughing at me. It's a terrible place.' Gryfflet's teeth were chattering as he spoke.

Now that the dragon's eyes were accustomed to the darkness, he could see that it was indeed a very black and frightening place. It was a deep cleft in the hill, leading down to the valley below, between high cliffs of stone. And under the cliffs were even darker hollows. It is called the Cheddar Gorge and you may see it to this day in the Mendip hills.

'Caves,' whispered Gryfflet. 'Full of bats.'

The dragon knew all about caves, for he lived in one in Cornwall, but he did not care for these ones, which looked unfriendly. 'Come on,' he said. 'We don't want to spend the night here, do we? Altogether too shut in.'

They began trudging up the long hill, Starlight and the heavier horse walking behind them. On top of the Mendips, a stiff wind was blowing and as they came out of the deep gorge on to the open down, it hit them in their faces and whipped round their legs.

'It's horrible up here,' groaned Gryfflet.

'It's more horrible down there,' retorted the dragon. 'Jump up and down, Gryfflet, while I think which way to go.'

Gryfflet obediently jumped up and down, his armour clattering like saucepans on a kitchen range. For a moment the dragon had a feeling of panic. I don't know the way to Ubley from here, he thought. I don't know the way by road.

Then he planted his four feet firmly on the grass and fought down his fears. 'I will be a brave dragon,' he muttered. 'I will not panic. Dragons Never Despair.' He lifted his head and snuffed the air and from the direction of his right front paw there seemed to come a pull, like the tug of the tide. 'This way,' he said confidently, and they set off again.

It was not far to Ubley Warren and before they arrived it grew lighter and the keen wind dropped. Night was fading into day, and the stars were growing pale. A few pink streaks appeared in the grey eastern sky. The dragon listened to poor Gryfflet telling him for at least the fourth time how he had ridden towards the clump of trees and how night had fallen and the clump had disappeared, and how without knowing what was happening he had found himself riding farther down and down into what seemed to be the centre of a mountain.

'Terrible,' murmured the dragon, sympathetically. 'I had quite a nasty time myself. No food.' But Gryfflet didn't seem to want to hear about the dragon's hungry walk.

At last they arrived at Ubley, and there were Wookey and Banwell, leaning on their picks, just about to go off to the mine for the morning's work.

'Ah, there you are!' cried Wookey, cheerfully. 'I got a bed ready for yon knight in my hut – first turn on the left and the third hut.'

'The Town Hall is ready for you,' said Banwell politely to the dragon. 'It is the only building large enough, I am afraid.'

The dwarfs had cleared the Town Hall of its chairs and spread mattresses on the floor so that the dragon could at least lay his head and shoulders down in comfort.

'I am afraid your back legs and tail will have to lie in the street,' explained Banwell, 'but I have set two watchers on guard over them and they will cover you up with rugs if it rains.'

'Thank you,' said the dragon and wondered if there was any breakfast. There was. It had been laid out on a table in front of the Town Hall, a bowl of porridge for Grifflet, a pail of porridge for the dragon and a basket of hay each for Grifflet's horse and Starlight.

'I wonder,' said the dragon, taking a breath half-way through his porridge, 'exactly how it was I heard Grifflet calling me.'

'The air is full of sounds,' answered Banwell, 'if your ears are quick enough to pick them up. Your ears aren't quite quick enough yet. What actually happened was, we heard the words carried on the air, and we – as it were – passed on what he was calling to you, passed it on loudly, so that you could hear.'

'I see,' said the dragon thoughtfully. 'I'd like to be better at it. It might be very useful.'

'You will have to train yourself,' said Banwell seriously.

'How?'

'You must listen hard for all the things you've never heard,' said the dwarf. 'You must listen for the fall of a leaf, for the whirr of a bird's wing in the air, for the clash of two grass blades against each other in a wind, for the tramp of a snail, for the cry of a snake, for the grind of a mole's teeth, for the rustle of two grains of sand against two other grains of sand.'

'And if I did this, if I trained my ears,' said the dragon,

'I might hear my old friend the giant boy, David, calling me?'

'Your friend David?' asked Banwell.

The dragon then told the dwarfs the story of his meeting with the giant Jubeance and his wife, of his year in King Arthur's kitchens, and of his desire to find the giant cook and restore him to his sorrowing parents. Many other dwarfs gathered round to hear the story, and when it was over, there was a deep silence. At last an elderly and spectacled dwarf approached the dragon, and after announcing himself – 'Doctor Harptree, at your service' – he went on: 'It would be – errm – of great medical interest to me – errm – to take the pulse of a young giant such as this. I should like to compare the rate of his pulse with, say, a dwarf's or a dragon's – errm.'

'His waist measurements would be interesting,' observed another dwarf, licking his stubby pencil.

'And there's the question of his appetite,' added Cheddar.

'I suggest,' interrupted the dragon, 'that we find the giant first. Wouldn't that be simpler?'

The dwarfs were very struck with this idea.

'I will leave in the morning,' went on the dragon, and he looked round for Gryfflet, but the knight, overcome by lack of sleep, had dozed off with his head on the table.

The dwarfs looked very crestfallen. 'Leave us?' they cried. 'Such an interesting and unusual creature! Dear, dear! Sad loss to scientific knowledge!'

Suddenly a voice said: 'I'd like to come with you, Dragon, if you'll take me.'

The speaker was Wookey, the little man with a face like brown leather, seamed and folded. The dragon recognized him as the dwarf who had offered to act as his guide when he was going to search for Gryfflet.

'Why do you want to come?' he asked.

Wookey hesitated. 'Two reasons,' he said, at last. 'I want to explore. I've a great desire to see more of England. And I am a maker of maps and I should like to see Wales and make one or two sketches for our Geographical Institute.'

The dragon wondered how Gryfflet would take to this idea. At first he humm'd and ha'd, and said gloomily, 'It'll mean another mouth to feed.' But the dragon pointed out that a dwarf ate extremely little, and in the end, remembering how he had been rescued, Gryfflet agreed that Wookey should come with them.

Next morning, they made ready to start. Starlight and Gryfflet's horse were groomed, Gryfflet's armour was polished (and written down piece by piece in a book by the chief armourer), and at last they were ready. Wookey appeared with an axe stuck through his belt, a haversack full of provisions, a large basket of eggs, and a pair of climbing boots slung round his neck by the laces.

'One must be ready for anything,' he said.

Banwell came and shook the dragon's paw. 'Don't forget,' he said. 'With practice you will be able to hear those who call you. Listen every day for the sounds you never hear, for the brush of the fly's wing on the bark of a tree, for the rattle of a woodlouse's scales, for the snore of a slumbering worm. When you can hear all these, you will be able to hear every sound in the world.' He smiled, almost kindly, and not at all scientifically, at the dragon. 'If *you* are ever in trouble,' he added, 'call on us and we shall hear you and come to your help if we can.'

It was a fine May morning when they set out from

Ubley Warren on their travels to find the giant cook.
Priddy had said that the dwarfs might be able to help
them in their search, but the dragon did not feel that he
was much further on. He still had no idea who the
mysterious lady in the coach was, and the only definite
thing that the dwarfs had told him was the direction in
which Wales lay.

'Follow the Mendip hills to the end,' they had said,
'turn north-west and you will come to a great river.
Cross it, and you will soon be in Wales.'

So off they went, the dragon plodding along on his
great feet, Grymflet sitting on his ambling horse and the
dwarf leading Starlight and singing little songs to himself:

> 'I was born and bred in Wookey Hole,
> I can see in the dark like a mole,
> I can see in the dark like a bat
> So you'd better be careful what you're at.'

'Can you really see in the dark?' asked Grymflet.

'I certainly can,' replied Wookey.

'It might come in useful,' remarked Grymflet.

'Sh-h-h,' said the dragon, frowning.

'Why should I shush?' asked the knight.

'I'm practising something.'

Grymflet sighed. He watched the dragon and this is what
he saw: the dragon had stopped a little way ahead of them
and put his right ear to the ground. He seemed to be
listening intently. Then he changed over to the other ear.
He shook his head, and reared up on his hind legs. He
stood there, his head high in the air.

'You look like a stone figure on a gatepost,' remarked
Grymflet.

The dragon cast a ferocious look in his direction.

'Sorry,' said the knight, humbly. 'I forgot.'

The dragon listened intently. A hawk was hovering in the sky, and the dragon gazed fixedly at it as though he had never seen one before. Gryfflet looked anxiously at Wookey. 'What's the matter with him?' he whispered.

'I think he's practising.'

'Practising what?'

'Listening.'

The dragon let out a puff of green smoke and put his forepaws down again to the ground. 'No good,' he said, looking very discouraged. 'I didn't hear a thing except you two whispering.'

'Never mind,' said Wookey. 'You've only just begun.'

Gryfflet took out a handkerchief and blew his nose loudly. 'I wish I could understand you,' he said, in a tearful voice. 'You're the oddest dragon I've ever known.'

'I'm the *only* dragon you've ever known,' corrected the dragon.

'You weren't like this in Cornwall,' complained Gryfflet. 'Things were simple then. Just eating and battles.'

'Boring,' said the dragon, waving a paw. 'Boring. This is far more interesting.'

'I feel left out,' said Gryfflet and wiped away a tear.

The dragon suddenly looked round at him. 'Did you sniff?' he asked eagerly.

'No, I don't think so,' said Gryfflet.

'Well,' said the dragon, stopping dead. 'That must have been your tears that I heard running down your cheeks. Wookey, it's beginning to come! I'm learning!'

Gryfflet reined in his horse. 'If you don't tell me what all this is about,' he said, bitterly, 'I shall go home.'

The dragon said he was sorry, and he had not meant to

be unkind, and he explained to Grÿfflet that he was practising what Banwell had told him: how to listen to the sounds he had never heard, like the breath of a fly. 'And now,' cried the dragon triumphant, 'I have heard a tear falling – your tears, Grÿfflet! Plop! Plop! Plop!'

That made Sir Grÿfflet very proud, for he felt he was adding to scientific knowledge; and, after that, he used to stand patiently while the dragon listened for the clash of two grass blades, or the tramp of a snail's feet as it walked across the path in front of him.

CHAPTER TEN

Adventures on the Road

ON the third day, they reached the far western end of the Mendip hills. There was the sea, and two rocky islands just off the coast. Far across the water was a dusky mass of hills.

'That's Wales,' said Wookey.

They all stood and looked at it for some time without speaking. Then Grytflet said, in a subdued voice, 'It looks very far away.'

'It is,' said Wookey carelessly. 'Miles. But we needn't cross the channel here. We'll go farther north, and cross by the ferry where the river is narrower.'

'Let's have an early supper,' suggested the dragon. 'Up here, where we can look at Wales.'

So they sat down in the golden light of the late afternoon, and unpacked the food. Starlight and Grytflet's

charger were turned on to a patch of grass to feed, and
Wookey went off with his axe to get firewood. He disappeared down a deep cleft near the path, a swallet-hole, full
of dry brushwood and stunted trees. The dragon filled a
saucepan from the water-jar, and placed in it seven eggs.

'One for Wookey, two for Grymflet, four for me,' he
said, thoughtfully, as he put them in. 'It was kind of
Banwell to add a basket of eggs. It makes a change from
walnuts and cheese.' He hesitated for a moment. 'One for
Wookey, two for Grymflet, *five* for me,' he said. Then he
counted what was left in the basket. There were sixteen
eggs. Just right, he thought. Eight tomorrow, eight the
day after. Perhaps we'll be able to get some more from a
farm. We might make scrambled eggs tomorrow. He
paused. 'And an omelette on Thursday,' he added, aloud.
'We could put some cheese in the omelette and that
would make it go farther.'

'Don't let's go any farther,' said Grymflet, hastily, who
had only heard the last part of the sentence.

'Silly old knight,' said the dragon. 'I was only talking
about food.'

'Oh,' said Grymflet. 'When will it be ready?'

'When we've got a fire going and boiled the eggs,'
answered the dragon. 'Where is Wookey, by the way?'

They looked round, and there was no sign of him.

'The sun's much lower,' said Grymflet, anxiously. 'You
know, he's been gone about half an hour.'

'Have I really been thinking about food for half an
hour?' asked the dragon, surprised. He looked about him.
'Grymflet,' he said, 'what's that?'

From the deep hollow, down which the dwarf had
gone for the firewood, a thin blue streak of smoke was
rising.

They gazed at it for a moment, puzzled.

'He can't have lit the fire down there,' said the dragon. 'Grymflet, suppose something's happened to him? We must go after him.'

'What, into that nasty, dark swallet-hole?' protested the knight, turning pale.

The dragon glared at Gryfflet. 'It was into that swallet-hole that he went, so that's where I'm going to look for him,' he said, rather sharply. 'You can look up and down the open path, where he isn't, if you prefer.'

Gryfflet's eyes filled with tears. 'I can't help not being brave,' he said. 'I wasn't meant to be a knight, and I hate swallet-holes. But I shall come with you, all the same.'

The dragon patted his shoulder. 'I knew you would,' he said. 'And you *are* brave, but I shall go first. And if there is anything unpleasant there I shall bite it. Draw your sword, so that you can cut off its head afterwards, whatever it is.'

The dragon started to climb down the narrow, rocky cleft. It was dark and damp, and the brushwood was thick and full of winding creepers. The dragon pushed them aside, but they caught on his fins, and progress was slow. The swallet-hole grew narrower and deeper. There was a faint smell of smoke, rather pleasant, as though sweet-smelling herbs were being burnt. Suddenly they heard sounds ahead of them, a crackle of broken twigs, stones dislodged and rattling against the rocky sides of the cleft. The dragon stopped.

'Gryfflet,' he said. 'Stop up your ears. I'm going to let out a roar, just to frighten whoever it is.'

Gryfflet stuffed his fingers in his ears, and the dragon opened his jaws and bellowed. It was a terrible sound and in that narrow cleft it echoed from side to side and thundered over their heads. At last it died away into silence and a small rough voice near by said angrily: 'No need to deafen a body.'

It was the dwarf.

'Are you all right?' cried the dragon. 'You're not hurt?'

'Only my ears,' retorted Wookey. 'They're deafened for life, I shouldn't wonder. I've found something interesting.'

'You've been gone a long time,' remarked the dragon. 'We were getting very anxious and alarmed.'

'We braved the terrors of this terrible swallet-hole, just to find you,' cried Grifflet through chattering teeth.

'Terrors? What terrors?' cried Wookey, scornfully. 'Why, bless you, it's no more than a girt old swallet-hole. Lammock's Lair they call this one.'

'Maybe,' said Grifflet. 'Never mind whose lair it is. We're not used to swallet-holes.'

'It's a deep one, it's true,' said Wookey. 'Now listen, the pair of you, did you see any smoke just now?'

'We did,' answered the dragon.

'Well,' said the dwarf. 'When I came down here to get the brushwood, I smelt a faint smell of burning, a smell of hot wood-ash, and right at the bottom of the swallet-hole, in the entrance to Lammock's Lair, were the ashes of a fire still smouldering. I kicked them and they flared up and made the smoke that you must have seen. They smelt sweet, as though someone had strewn herbs on them. I looked round but I couldn't see anyone, and there were no creatures to ask. It was still too light for owls or bats to be awake.'

'It's getting dark now,' observed Grifflet, looking up.

Above them, the narrow patch of blue sky which

showed between the walls of the swallet-hole had turned to deep violet.

'Can't we leave whatever it is until tomorrow?' asked the knight, shivering slightly.

'Yes,' agreed the dragon, 'is there any point *now*, when we ought to be having supper?'

'Aha!' said Wookey, mysteriously. 'Oho! I think there *is* a point. In the cave someone has dropped a little book. It is labelled: *RECIPES. VOLUME TWO.*'

'Cooking recipes?' asked the dragon, eagerly. 'Something that would do for supper?'

'No,' answered Wookey patiently, 'not cooking recipes. *Spells.* I haven't had time or light to read them properly, but I did see one, and it was headed – just a minute, let's see if I can read it.'

He opened the book, turned over a few pages and peered at it.

' "Giants",' he read, and paused. The dragon and Gryfflet looked at each other.

' "Giants",' Wookey went on, ' "Important spell for turning back into a giant any of the following objects:

    1.   A windmill.
    2.   An oak tree.
    3.   A stone gate-post."

Now, what shall we do? Climb out and read these spells while it's light enough, or go down and explore the cave?'

'Climb out,' replied Gryfflet, at once. 'I'm sure that would be much the best.'

'I don't,' said Wookey, emphatically. 'If anyone knows what happened in that cave, it'll be an owl or possibly a bat. If she *has* – whoever she is – turned David into a windmill or an oak tree or a stone gate-post, then we want to know which, and maybe someone down there will know. We ought to go and ask them now it's getting dark. Down we go. Follow me. It'll be no good tomorrow morning.'

He disappeared into the darkness and Grytflet rather unwillingly stumbled after the dragon. The swallet-hole ended in the black cave called Lammock's Lair, at the entrance to which could still be seen the faint red glow of a fire. There was a stir of wings and a bat flittered by. Grytflet ducked.

'Now this is where your listening practice will come in, Dragon,' said Wookey. 'The voice of a bat is too high for ordinary ears to hear. I can hear it, of course, because my ears aren't ordinary, and perhaps you can now, after all your practice. Listen, I'll call them.'

Wookey put two fingers in his mouth and produced a soft, very high whistle, almost a squeak. Two or three bats flew out and wheeled over their heads in the gloom. Wookey whistled again. One bat left the others and clung to a tree, its tiny clawed feet grasping a small branch.

'Listen,' whispered the dwarf. The dragon strained his ears. In the silence he could hear a tiny, high-pitched voice. It said: 'D'you want anything, Dwarf?'

Wookey called again, three questioning notes.

'Oh, yes,' squeaked the bat. 'Oh, most certainly.'

Whistle, whistle, went Wookey's pursed lips.

'Two days ago,' answered the bat.

'Pooee, pooee, pooee-ee-ee?' queried the dwarf.

'A lady and a great big man,' said the bat. 'Biggest I ever saw.'

'Pooeee?'

'She boiled a pot over a fire, and dropped things into it. Then she fed this giant fellow out of a ladle.'

'Pooee-ee-ee-ee?'

'Nothing,' answered the bat, and wheeled over their heads several times. 'She said it would take a week to work. Do stamp out the fire, Dwarf, the smoke gets in our eyes. Most unpleasant it is.'

He flew off and joined his companions, who were circling up and down the narrow cleft in search of their evening meal.

'Could you hear what he said?' asked Wookey.

'Most of it,' answered the dragon, with pride. He felt that his listening practice had been rewarded already.

They stamped out the fire, and the dragon promised to tell Gryfflet what he had heard, as they climbed up the swallet-hole. It was dark now. They lit a fire and boiled the eggs and ate their supper by the light of the embers.

'I don't see that we're any better off,' said Gryfflet gloomily.

'Oh yes, we are,' retorted Wookey. 'She's worked a spell on him. She's turned him into either a windmill or an oak tree or a stone gate-post. I suppose the spell takes a week to work because he's so big.'

'I suppose so,' agreed the dragon. 'The trouble is that there aren't any windmills round here, but there are quite a lot of stone gate-posts, and there are *thousands* of oak trees. How are we to know which is poor David?'

But Wookey was thumbing over the pages of *Volume Two*.

'Look!' he cried. 'This is a very special spell book. It's a turning back book. Nothing else. Only spells for turning things back.'

'What d'you mean?' asked Gryfflet.

'Why, don't you see? *Volume One* must contain the spells she actually uses for turning things into other things. There are spells here for turning things back into their right shapes. Listen: "Spell for turning coachman back into knight. Spell for turning pig back into horse. Spell for turning peacock back into princess." My! she must work some pretty nasty spells on people.'

'I wonder who she is?' mused the dragon. 'Some witch, I suppose.'

'Listen to this one!' cried Wookey, bending near the fire to see the words. 'Oh, do blow up the fire a bit. I can hardly see.'

'Here's a beam from my eyes,' said the dragon, turning his yellow eyes like torches upon the small black book.

' "Spell, very special",' Wookey read out. ' "My private spell for turning myself back into myself." '

There was silence for a moment.

'Yes,' said the dragon. 'But we still don't know *who* she is, do we?'

'Wait a minute!' cried the dwarf, turning the pages quickly back to the beginning. 'Why, oh, why didn't I look at the inside of the cover before. It may have her name. Yes! Listen to this!' He read out to the others the inscription, written in faded ink, on the fly-leaf of *Volume Two*. ' "To my dear little Morgan on her tenth birthday, from her loving old Nurse." '

Grufflet snatched the book from the dwarf. 'I know who she is!' he cried. 'She's Morgan le Fay. *You* know, Dragon, daughter of King Leodegrance – King Arthur's half-sister, that's who she is!'

'Grufflet,' said the dragon, solemnly. 'I am glad we had such a wise and knowledgeable knight with us. Without you, we should never have got any further. Of course, that is who she is. I have heard of her, often, in the kitchens.'

They were all very excited at this, and the dragon's yellow eyes glowed even more brightly.

'Well,' said Wookey, at last, 'if she's turned herself into something, she'll want this book back, won't she – unless, of course, she knows her own spell by heart, and I doubt if she does. It's a very long one. A whole page. We've simply got to find her as well as David. Then we'll see!'

Tired out, the three adventurers lay back on the soft turf, and in the dying warmth of the fire, they fell asleep, the black *Volume Two* under Wookey's head.

Next day, they went on, they met no one, and though

they talked a great deal about the Book of Spells, *Volume Two*, they never arrived at any conclusion about poor David, who might be a windmill or an oak tree or a stone gate-post. In the evening, Wookey cut firewood with his axe, and they ate scrambled eggs and cheese and apples, and slept again under the bright stars, round the warm ashes of the fire. And so it went on for two or three days and nights more. Gryfflet began to enjoy the life.

'Rather like gypsies,' he said. 'It's wonderful to be free. No battles. No dreary long feasts. No practising in the tilting with those fearful lances. Peaceful, isn't it?'

The country was deeply wooded now, and they rode along quiet, forest rides, shaded from the sun, and dappled green and gold. Gryfflet was so happy that he wished it might never end, but the dragon was restless and anxious.

'This is a quest,' he said sternly to Gryfflet, one morning when the knight was basking under an oak tree and refused to get up. 'This very oak tree might be poor David.'

There was not a sound in the depth of the woods, except the song of birds and a cuckoo calling.

Suddenly Wookey, who was plaiting Starlight's mane and weaving grasses among the plaits, called out: 'Dragon! I can hear something! Listen!'

The dragon placed a heavy paw on Gryfflet's shoulder to keep him quiet and cocked his great green ears. He *could* hear something. It was faint – a kind of clatter, which reminded him of the noises he used to hear in the kitchens, saucepans clinking, lids falling to the ground, spoons scraping on pans.

'It's the clash of armour! There's a fight somewhere! Come on!' shouted Wookey. He seized Gryfflet's horse.

'I'll sit in front of you,' he said. 'Up with you, Sir Knight!'

Reluctantly, Grylflet pushed his helmet on to his head and climbed into the saddle. The dwarf scrambled on in front of him, and seized Starlight by the bridle rein. They set off as fast as they could, which was not at a very remarkable speed, for Grylflet's horse was a heavy charger and the dragon could only go at a trot. Every now and again they paused to take their direction. The green silence of the forest closed round them and they listened. In a moment, Wookey and the dragon picked up the clang of arms, and after a short while, even Grylflet could hear it.

'We're getting near,' panted the dragon. Suddenly they came out into a wide, sunlit clearing. A man in a leather tunic, and steel leg-pieces, was lying dead on the ground, his helmet cleft in two pieces, his sword broken off at the hilt. But two more ruffians were attacking a tall knight, in full armour. He was laying about him with his sword and although they were two to one, so tremendous were his sword blows that the two of them cried 'Mercy! mercy!' and turned to fly.

It was just at this point that the dragon set foot in the clearing, and the two men, seeing a dragon barring their path, howled with terror and ran back into the clearing again. Desperately they fought against the single knight, but they were overcome and he slew them, one after the other. Then he lifted his helmet to mop the sweat off his face, and the dragon recognized him. It was Bewmains!

'You came just at the right moment,' cried Bewmains, and seized the dragon by both paws. Great was their pleasure at the meeting. The dragon was longing to hear his adventures, but Bewmains was in a hurry. 'I have rescued a knight from these villains,' he explained, 'but he lies bound near by. I must go and unbind him.'

'And your lady?' asked the dragon. 'The lady for whom you undertook the quest?'

Bewmains looked rueful. 'She doesn't like me,' he said. 'She still treats me as a kitchen boy.'

The dragon was indignant. 'Leave her!' he cried.

'No,' answered Bewmains. 'I have undertaken this quest on her behalf, to rescue her sister from the Castle Perilous. I must carry it out, even if she hates me to the end. If you come with me, you will see how she treats me, but you must say nothing.'

So, for a short distance, they travelled together through the forest and the dragon told Bewmains about the dwarfs, and Bewmains told the dragon of the adventures he had had and how he had found a knight bound and held by six thieves, who were threatening to kill him. Three he had slain but the other three had fled and he had pursued them into this clearing where the dragon had found them fighting.

'Surely the lady will know now what a true and brave knight you are?' said the dragon, full of admiration.

Bewmains shrugged his shoulders. 'We shall see,' he said.

The knight, still bound, was lying under a tree, a few miles away, and near by was the lady whom Bewmains served. Bewmains soon untied the ropes which bound the knight and he rose stiffly to his feet and thanked his rescuer warmly.

'Sir,' he said, 'I owe my life to you. What is your name?'

'I cannot tell you my name,' said Bewmains. 'I come from the north, and am the son of royal parents. I serve that lady yonder and ride on a quest to rescue her sister.'

'Do not believe him!' called out the lady, at once. 'He is no knight. He is a kitchen boy from King Arthur's kitchens. His clothes smell of grease. He is no more than a turnspit and a ladle-washer.'

The knight looked puzzled. 'Lady,' he said, 'this knight is no kitchen boy. He has fought valiantly and slain six ruffians. He has saved my life.'

The lady laughed very scornfully at this. 'It was nothing more than good luck,' she said. 'I would be ashamed to owe my life to a scullion.'

'None the less, I do owe it to him,' answered the knight, 'and care not who he be. I beg you both to come to my castle and take dinner with me, and rest there for the night.'

'Fie! Fie! You insult me if you think that I should sit down at table with a kitchen boy!'

'Good Sir,' said Bewmains. 'It were best we went on our way. We will leave you. Let her say what she will, I have undertaken to King Arthur to make this quest and I shall pursue it to the end, no matter what scorn she pours upon me.'

At this, the knight bade them both farewell, and rode sadly away. The lady mounted her horse and, casting a scornful glance at the dragon, said: 'I heard tell of this kitchen beast – some overgrown dog, I suppose – when I came to King Arthur's court. It seems that half the kitchen staff go on quests these days. And who is yon knight?' She pointed at Gryfflet. 'The head cook, dressed up in armour?'

Poor Gryfflet dropped his sword in his agitation.

'He cannot even hold his sword,' said the lady, with a peal of laughter.

'We must go on,' said Bewmains sadly. 'We have to cross the great river, and go north where, on the borders of Wales and England, stands the Castle Perilous. It is there that her sister is besieged.'

'The river!' cried the dragon. 'We have to cross it, too, for the only clue we have about giant David is that he is somewhere in Wales.'

So they agreed to travel on together towards the river crossing. The dragon, of course, walked with Bewmains, and they talked and laughed pleasantly together as they used to in the old kitchen days. But it was not to be for long.

'When we come to the ferry, we must part,' said Bewmains. 'I told you before that quests cannot be undertaken together. You have yours and I have mine.'

'Why do you put up with her?' asked the dragon. 'She taunts you and provokes you all the time. If I were in your paws – your shoes, I mean – I should have nipped her sharply in the leg by now, if not bitten her head off.'

'On a quest,' answered Bewmains, 'everything one meets must be endured. Certainly, it is hard to bear her insolent words, but if I *do* bear them, and if I release her sister from her prison in the Castle Perilous, I shall have achieved my adventure, and proved myself a true knight.'

'No one who knew you could possibly think you a common kitchen boy,' said the dragon, proudly.

'Kitchen boys can be as brave as knights,' said Bewmains, 'and knights can have the cowardly hearts of rabbits. Some people may despise even dragons, and think they are just creatures who eat maidens, but I know better.'

The dragon blushed with pleasure, for there is no praise in the world so sweet as the praise of someone you love and admire, as the dragon loved and admired Bewmains.

At last they came to a great river and there was a barge to take them over, but, guarding it, stood two knights who barred the way.

'Well, kitchen boy,' called out the lady, 'will you make these two knights give place to you, or shall we all turn back again?'

'Nay,' cried Bewmains. 'I would not turn back were there six of them.'

'Perhaps Sir Gryfflet here will help you,' suggested the lady, at which the poor knight began to tremble.

'The adventure is mine,' cried Bewmains, angrily. 'Sir Gryfflet must keep to his own quest.'

'Ah well,' said the damsel. 'He will be my protector when yon knights have tossed you into the water.'

Then Bewmains rode fiercely against the two knights, and they began to give ground before him. One received such a buffet that he had to take off his helmet to get a breath of fresh air and restore himself. Bewmains then drove the second one right into the river. They fought on, waist deep in the water, their horses' hooves slipping on the stony bottom, till their spears broke in their hands. Then they drew their swords, and smote eagerly at each other. At last Bewmains gave the other such a blow on his helmet that the knight was stunned and fell back into the river and was swept away and drowned. Meanwhile the other knight had recovered and put his helmet on again, and as soon as Bewmains turned his horse and spurred him out of the water, at once the knight fell upon him. For a few moments it looked as if Bewmains was hard pressed, and the damsel could hardly conceal her delight. But at last he made a thrust at the enemy and caught him off his guard. His sword point entered a joint of the armour and the knight fell to the ground, dead.

Bewmains rode up to the damsel, and bade her take her place in the barge, to be rowed across the river.

'Alas,' she sighed, 'that two such good knights should be slain by a kitchen boy. I suppose you think you have done bravely? It is not so at all. The first knight's horse slipped – I saw it myself – and that is why he was drowned, and as for the second, you hit him from behind, a cowardly blow, and slew him most unfairly.'

'Damsel,' said Bewmains, patiently, 'you may say what you will. I care nothing, so long as I may rescue your sister.' Then he called Priddy, his dwarf, and they said their farewells.

'I will send the ferryman back for you,' said Bewmains. 'The time has come to go our separate ways. Good fortune to your quest!'

'Good fortune to yours!' cried the dragon. 'We shall meet again.'

'Perhaps,' said Bewmains, rather sadly, as he followed the damsel into the barge. 'Perhaps we may, but there is no certainty. Good-bye, old Dragon.'

The dragon and his party stood on the bank, and watched the barge slowly moving over the water, carrying Bewmains and his disagreeable lady. Then they sat down by the river-side and waited for the ferry-boat to come back across the river. Suddenly, they heard a commotion on the far bank, and, looking across, they could just see a group of figures on the other side. Something large was being hauled aboard the barge. There was a long delay. Gryfflet grew more and more dismal.

'I hate the water,' he groaned. 'I shall be sea-sick, I am certain.'

'Nonsense,' cried the dragon. 'It's a river. Who ever heard of anyone being river-sick?'

'I shall be,' said Gr, said Gryfflet.

'Think about something else,' advised the dragon. 'I tell you what, I'll practise listening and you can watch me. That will take your mind off the river.'

'What will you listen for?' asked Gryfflet.

'I'll listen for the little fishes as they brush against the reeds,' replied the dragon, and with that he planted his front paws firmly in the shallow edge of the river, and bent his ear to the surface of the water.

This certainly took Gryfflet's thoughts off his own fears. He was all anxiety for the dragon. He beckoned Wookey to him. 'I'm certain he'll fall in,' he whispered fearfully.

'Never mind. He can swim,' answered the dwarf.

'He might get caught in the weeds and drown,' persisted Gryfflet.

The dragon looked up. 'I can hear something,' he said, with excitement.

Wookey and Gryfflet gathered round him, on the sandy river edge.

'What can you hear?' asked Wookey.

'A sort of *swish, swish*,' said the dragon. 'It must be the fish.' He bent his head again. 'It's getting louder,' he said. '*Swish, swish, swish. Swirl, swirl, swirl.* It must be a huge fish.'

'Perhaps it's a whale,' said Gryfflet and backed away.

'You don't get whales in rivers,' said Wookey, patiently and politely. He was fond of Gryfflet and did not wish to appear scornful, but he secretly thought him very ignorant.

'*Swish, swish*,' said the dragon again, listening intently.

Suddenly there was a cry of 'Ahoy!' They all looked up, and there, a few yards from the bank, was the ferry-boat.

The dragon looked very disappointed. 'It must have been the boat coming towards us that I heard,' he said with a sigh. Then he looked again and added with excitement: 'Look what's aboard the boat!'

On the deck stood a black coach, and painted on its door was a golden shield with three black cooking-pots emblazoned upon it.

CHAPTER ELEVEN

The Ferry

SITTING inside the coach was a hideous old woman. On the bridge of her hooked nose, the knobbly bone stuck out like a wart. Her eyes were deeply sunken under bushy eyebrows. Thin grey wisps of hair feathered out from under her broad hat, which was skewered to her head by a gigantic hat-pin, made in the shape of a spider. The coach was drawn by a black horse, and driven by a red-faced, unhappy-looking coachman, to whom the old woman kept shouting, leaning out of the coach window as she did so. As the ferry-boat reached the shore, her words became clear.

'I must have it! I must have it! Coachman, you are to crawl back to Camelot on your hands and knees looking for it. It's clear I dropped it somewhere. If you don't find it, I shall have you imprisoned for life. I shall have your head chopped off. I shall have you boiled in lead.'

By now the boat was at the landing stage. The ferryman had steered its flat, square nose on to the bank, and the coachman was guiding the black horse towards dry land. The coat of arms on the door was now very plain to see.

'Black cooking-pots,' observed the dragon, thoughtfully. 'Black, three-legged cooking-pots. That is what I thought I saw on the coach that drove away with David, and that's what was on the coach that stole poor Martha's son, Giles, or so the farm-boy said. I smell a rat – more than one rat.'

The old woman was now leaning out of her coach again, her eyes blazing. 'Drive on slowly,' she cried, 'and mind you look carefully, every inch of the way.'

Wookey stepped forward suddenly. 'Madam,' he began, politely. 'I think I overheard you say that you had lost something.'

'Have you picked it up?' demanded the old woman eagerly.

'I might have,' answered Wookey, calmly. 'It depends what it is. I pick up a lot of things.' Then, '*Get on to the barge now, all of you,*' he added in a whisper to the dragon.

The dragon pushed the unwilling Grylflet and the two horses towards the barge.

'What *have* you picked up?' asked the old woman.

Wookey felt in his pockets. 'Well,' he said, slowly, 'I've got a – walnut.'

'Fool!' screamed the old woman.

Wookey felt again. 'A lump of sheep's wool,' he went on. 'Let me see . . .'

'Idiot! Have you a *book*?'

'I might have,' said Wookey and began to move towards the barge.

'Give it to me!' she screamed, almost beside herself, trying to open the door of her carriage which was stuck.

'Coachman, let me out! Let me out! He's got my book! He's got my *Volume Two*, and the door's stuck!' She tugged at it furiously till the coach rocked to and fro.

By this time, Wookey was standing on the flat prow of the barge. The dragon, Grylflet and the two horses were all safely on board. 'Push off!' said Wookey to the ferryman, adding, 'but don't go too far out. I want to continue this conversation.'

'Come back! Come back! My book!' screamed the old woman. The coachman had got the door open by now and she was hobbling at a remarkable pace towards the bank.

'Would it be a Book of Spells: *Volume Two*?' asked Wookey, innocently.

'Yes, yes, that's it!' And she danced up and down on the edge of the river, her black clothes flapping round her like raven's wings.

'Now, what would a dear old lady like you want with spells?' asked the dwarf.

'It's – it's *my* book. You have no right to it.'

'But this book must belong to Morgan le Fay,' said the dragon. He took the volume from Wookey and looked at the beginning. 'It says here: "To my dear little Morgan on her tenth birthday".'

There was a moment's silence, and then the old woman screeched: 'I *am* Morgan le Fay – can't you see? – only I've changed my shape.'

'Ah,' said Wookey, nodding wisely, 'and you need page twenty-nine to tell you how to turn yourself back again, is that right?'

'Yes,' answered the witch, looking very sulky.

'Dear me, can't you remember your own spell?'

'No, I can't. I've got a very bad memory,' said the witch, peevishly, 'and it's a terribly long spell.'

'Yes,' agreed Wookey, counting down the page. 'Seventeen ingredients. It *is* long, isn't it? Tut, tut! What it is to have a bad memory. Shall we give her back her book, Dragon?'

'We-e-ell,' the dragon scratched his scaly nose with one paw. 'We might . . . and then again we might not.'

'Give it back! Give it back, you villains!' cried the old woman.

'Ask nicely,' said the dragon, frowning.

'Please,' begged Morgan le Fay.

'The only thing is,' said the dragon, 'we might need it ourselves. Now, suppose you tell me just what you have done with my friend David, the giant cook, then I might think about giving it back.'

'I won't!' screamed the witch.

'Ferryman,' said the dragon, waving a paw. 'Take us across.'

The barge began to move away from the bank.

'Oh, come back, come back!' called the wicked Morgan le Fay. 'Give me back my book and I'll tell you where he is.'

The ferryman stopped his oars.

'Well?' called Wookey.

'He's a – he's turned into a stone gate-post at the entrance to Castle Perilous,' cried Morgan le Fay, in desperation.

'Ah!' said the dragon. 'Castle Perilous. Off we go, ferryman!'

'But my book!' shrieked the witch.

'We'll give it back later. That's a promise,' called the dragon, and waved a friendly paw.

As the barge moved slowly across the river, the coach and the black dancing figure of the furious witch grew smaller and smaller on the bank. Just before she went out of sight altogether, they could see her climbing into the coach and driving off very fast in a northerly direction.

The ferryman shook his head. 'Off to Gloucester, that's what she is,' he said, 'to ford the river there. Then she'll drive down to Castle Perilous.'

'Can she get there before we do?' asked the dragon.

'She might,' answered the ferryman. 'You've a tidy way to go, and her route, though longer, is flatter. *And* she's in a coach. I wouldn't put it past her to arrive before you.'

'Can you tell us the way to Castle Perilous?' asked Wookey.

'Aye, I know these parts well,' answered the ferryman. 'I can tell you. When we get over to the far bank, take the road west and follow it through the forest. You'll come to a deep river but there's a bridge a little to the north, at Monmouth Castle. Cross there, and go up past the castle. Take the right fork, then the left, and travel on till you come to the third river, the River Usk. Follow that river in a northerly direction, against the current. Two days' journey should bring you to Castle Perilous. And rather you should go there than I, for I hear 'tis held by a terrible, fierce knight.'

At this moment there was a crash. The dragon jumped. 'What was that?' he asked.

'Something amiss with yon knight of yours,' observed the ferryman, and plied his oar stolidly, without taking further notice.

The dragon hurried over to Gryfflet, who was lying full length in the bottom of the boat, breathing heavily. The dragon and Wookey loosed the knight's helmet, and slipped it off, so that he could breathe more easily.

'What's the matter, Gryfflet?' asked the dragon, patting the knight's hand affectionately with his paw. 'Are you ill?'

'It's partly the boat,' whispered Gryfflet, 'and then I heard about Castle Perilous and the terrible fierce knight, and something seemed to come over me.'

'My poor Gryfflet,' said the dragon, sympathetically. 'Have a walnut. It will make you feel much better.'

He pulled two or three walnuts out of Starlight's pannier, and cracked the shells in his strong paws.

'There you are,' he said. 'Eat them up.'

Gryfflet chewed the nuts slowly. 'If I could have some water,' he faltered.

The dragon picked up the knight's helmet, and dipped it in the river, scooping up some water. Gryfflet sipped it gratefully, and the colour began to come back into his cheeks. 'Are we nearly there?' he asked.

'Just coming up to the bank,' called the ferryman, cheerfully.

Within a few minutes, they were on dry land again. They bought fresh supplies of food from the ferryman's wife, who lived in a cottage on this side of the river, and, after packing Starlight's panniers, Gryfflet climbed again on to his horse and they set out on their journey to Castle Perilous.

They crossed the bridge at Monmouth, and took the right fork, and then the left, and after three days they reached the River Usk, and there the journey might have ended for good, for a terrible thing happened – the dragon fell in the river (while doing some listening practice) and was quickly washed downstream by the current. Gryfflet and Wookey were almost frantic with alarm and despair. However, after rolling over and over like an empty barrel, the dragon was at last checked by a fallen willow which was lying across the river from bank to bank. Somewhat bruised and shaken, he pulled himself on to the edge, covered with weed, and snorting out water and green smoke – a kind of emerald steam. He had to be revived with a double helping of cheese, apples and walnuts. Gryfflet wanted to stop and boil a pannikin of milk for him, to keep the cold out, but the dragon insisted on hurrying forward.

'Time is getting short,' he said, 'and if Morgan le Fay reaches the castle before we do, who knows what fresh spells she may work on poor David? I shan't catch cold if I hurry.'

So he plodded on, his great green body still dripping with river water, winding along like a snake. Gryfflet followed on his charger, his armour rusty with damp and his moustache and beard drooping and draggled, while Wookey brought up the rear, leading Starlight, whose panniers were now nearly empty. They were rather worried about food, especially the dragon. It was, therefore, with joy and relief that they saw before them, at the end of the day, the lights of a town, and towers, church spires, and roofs, gleaming in the evening light. Outside the town walls, in a broad meadow where the mists were already rising, stood tents, their brilliant colours lit up by the glare of innumerable bonfires. As they drew near, they could hear music and the noise of merriment. Round them lay the silent mountains, black and grim, and the river glided cold beside their feet, but within the meadow all was bright and welcoming and they turned into the gate eagerly.

The field was newly mown, and smelt of fresh-cut grass. Around it stood the tents they had seen in the distance, more brilliant and gay than any of them had ever seen before. The men and women, too, who were thronging the wide lanes between the tents, and clustering round the bonfires, were dark-skinned and clothed in brightly coloured robes. Several of them approached the travellers, and as soon as they saw the great horned head of the dragon, they flung themselves upon their faces, not from fear, but from joy. They bowed their heads up and down and chanted words in a strange tongue. The dragon was extremely pleased, but Sir Gryfflet was nervous.

'They may be cannibals,' he whispered, anxiously.

'Nonsense!' said the dragon. 'They are obviously dragon-worshippers. I am delighted with them.'

At last the chief among them rose to his feet and cried: 'Noble Dragon, come with us to our master, Sir Persaunte. Never in all the years we have lived in this strange, cold, northern land have we been honoured by a visit from a royal dragon. Tell us what brings you here. Are you from far eastern climes?'

'No,' answered the dragon. 'I am, of course, royal' – and he waved his paw graciously towards the group – 'but I come from the land of Cornwall.'

As they led the party through the tents, Wookey took out a notebook and asked questions, the answers to which he busily wrote down. He learned that they were Indians, and had been driven out of their country by a cruel warrior king. Sir Persaunte had become their leader and had brought them through many dangers and over many seas to the land of Britain, where they had settled peaceably in the mountains of Wales, built a city, and lived very happily – 'except for the cold,' added the chief of them, and all the Indians shuddered: 'Br-r-r-r!'

'What are all these tents for?' asked Gryfflet. 'Is there a war?'

'No,' answered the chief. 'We are holding our yearly tournament. There has been jousting and tilting for three days.'

By now, they had reached the centre of the meadow, where had been built an enormous bonfire on which was flaring up to the black sky a whole oak-tree, roots and

all. Its flames gave a light more brilliant than the sun, and
the dragon and his friends saw seated near it a splendidly
dressed knight, wearing a scarlet helmet, with gold
patterns embossed upon it. His tunic was so heavily
embroidered with gold thread that the colour beneath
it could not be seen, while his long close-fitting silk
trousers were of bright yellow. Hardly had they taken
in this strange sight – an Indian prince transported to
these wild Welsh hills – when their eyes fell upon his
companions and with a cry of joy, they ran forward to
greet – Bewmains! Great as was their amazement at
finding him here, it was as nothing to the amazement of
the Indian knight and his fellows when they beheld a
large green dragon, accompanied by a travel-stained
knight in rusty armour, and a dwarf three feet high,
embracing their honoured visitor.

After the friends had expressed their joy at meeting
again, Bewmains turned to his host. 'Sir Persaunte,' he
cried, 'I beg leave to present to you my old and trusted
friend, this noble Cornish dragon, together with his
equally honourable companion, Sir Gryfflet, one of King
Arthur's dearest knights; and, least in size but not in
worth, the dwarf, Wookey, who comes from a learned
and scientific community of dwarfs in the Mendip
hills.'

Sir Persaunte of India was most gracious to the strang-
ers. Wine-cups were filled, healths were drunk, and golden platters of delicious food were placed within reach of
them from which they could help themselves when they
wished. When the feast was over, they sat in the light of
the bonfire, and after the dragon had told Bewmains of
their adventures at the crossing, and of the meeting there

with Morgan le Fay, he begged the knight to tell him all that had befallen him since they had parted.

This was the tale Bewmains told.

After leaving the dragon, he had fought and won many a hard battle, but despite his noble and courageous deeds, the lady continued to insult him, until at last the young man said to her, in his ever courteous manner: 'Damsel, I pray you, insult me no more. When you see me beaten, or a coward, then you may bid me go from you.'

To this the damsel made a scornful reply and warned him that soon he must meet with a knight who would utterly overthrow him, for he was the greatest knight in the world except only King Arthur.

'It will be the more honour to me, then, to do battle with him,' replied Bewmains. And the lady laughed and curled her lip.

Now this knight was the Indian prince, Sir Persaunte, who was holding a tournament in the broad meadow, and challenging to combat every knight who came his way. When Bewmains saw him, in his splendid armour, standing amid his attendants in the pavilioned meadow he cried, 'Let him come and let him do his worst!'

The damsel saw that Bewmains was determined. She remembered all the insults she had heaped upon him, which he had borne so patiently, and at last she relented, and said to him, 'Sir, I marvel who you are, and of what noble family you were born. It must be that you are of gentle blood, for never did a woman treat a knight so shamefully as I have treated you, and yet you have borne it all without a word.'

Bewmains smiled a little at this, the first soft speech he had heard from his lady, and replied: 'Damsel, I never heeded your words, except to spur on my anger against my enemies. Therefore your unkind sayings did me good service in my battles.'

'Alas!' said the lady. 'Fair Bewmains, forgive me all I have said or done against you.'

'With all my heart,' said he.

Then Sir Persaunte of India spied them and after some high words, he rode against Bewmains and they fought an hour or more. At last, Bewmains smote Sir Persaunte on the helmet, and he fell grovelling to the earth. Then the knight leapt upon him and unlaced his helmet in order to slay him, but Sir Persaunte yielded and asked him mercy, and the damsel prayed him to save the Indian knight's life.

Bewmains was glad to spare it, for his enemy had proved a valiant fighter. So they went into Sir Persaunte's pavilion and drank wine and ate spiced cakes. After they were refreshed, Sir Persaunte promised Bewmains his homage and loyalty and a hundred knights to do him service. The damsel was glad to hear this, 'For,' she said, 'we shall need every help when we come to the Castle Perilous, where my sister Lyonesse lies besieged. The Red Knight of the Red Lands is the fiercest knight upon earth, and is served by a strong and terrible army.'

It was this same evening, after the combat of Bewmains and the Indian knight, that the dragon and his party arrived. They were eager to leave early the next morning, together with Bewmains and his lady. Before they left, however, Sir Persaunte warned Bewmains of the strength and valour of the Red Knight, who was laying siege to Castle Perilous. 'God save you, Bewmains,' he said, 'from that dangerous knight, for he doth great wrong to

the lady. Yet she is one of the fairest ladies in all the
world. Be ye strong and of a good heart. If you can match
that Red Knight, you shall be called one of the greatest
knights in all the world.'

'Sir,' said Bewmains, 'I would wish to win fame and
knighthood, and a place at the Round Table. I am come
of a goodly family. My father was noble, and if you and
my damsel Lynette, and you, Sir Gryfflet, and my old
friend Dragon, will keep my secret, I will tell you what kin
I come of.'

'We will not reveal it,' they all promised.

'Truly, then,' said he, 'my name is Gareth of Orkney.
King Lot was my father, and my mother is King Arthur's
sister. Her name is Dame Morgause. Sir Gawaine is my
brother, and also Sir Agravaine and Sir Gaheris, and I
am the youngest of them all, and have come unknown to
the court of the King, to win my knighthood.'

The dragon gazed proudly at his friend, and cast a
rather scornful glance at Lynette, who had the grace to
blush. 'I knew you were no kitchen boy,' he cried,
triumphantly.

CHAPTER TWELVE

Castle Perilous

ALTHOUGH both the dragon and Bewmains were seeking the Castle Perilous, they went by different roads. The reason for this was that the dragon dared not lose any more time. He must reach the stone gates before Morgan le Fay, therefore he had to go by the straightest and quickest route. They parted from Sir Persaunte the following morning, and Bewmains, with his escort of a hundred knights, moved slowly down the narrow lanes, while the dragon and his party hurried along the broad highway.

Sir Gryfflet now began to be extremely fearful. 'What if we should meet the Red Knight of the Red Lands?' he asked. 'No doubt he is accompanied by an army. They will account us enemies and attack us forthwith. They may even kill us.'

The dragon paused. 'What you say is not without wisdom,' he admitted. 'Wookey, what do you think?

Are we running into danger in approaching the Castle openly in this way?'

'I think we are,' answered Wookey.

The dragon sat down. 'I will make a plan,' he said. After a few minutes' silence, he looked round at his companions. 'We must camouflage ourselves,' he said. 'Tie green branches all over us, and then the Red Knight, if he sees us, will think we are a wood.'

'He will think we are a very strange wood,' observed Wookey, '– a few green branches walking along a road. Now I have another plan, Dragon.'

The dragon frowned. 'I like my plan best,' he said, quickly.

'You haven't heard mine,' objected Wookey.

'Let us hear it,' pleaded Sir Gryfflet. 'Perhaps we could use *both* plans.'

The dragon looked slightly better pleased. 'Well?' he said, rather reluctantly.

'My plan was this,' said Wookey. 'I am small and not easily noticed. Let me go forward and spy out the land. Let me find these gate-posts and see if we can get to them unobserved. In the meantime you and Sir Gryfflet and the horses can lie hidden here –'

'Covered with branches!' exclaimed the dragon, eagerly.

'Well, yes, you two can be covered with branches, if you like,' added Wookey, hastily.

'It's a good plan,' said the dragon, and Gryfflet heaved a sigh of relief.

So Wookey disappeared across the fields, and the dragon and Gryfflet tethered the horses where they could crop peacefully. Then they cut down a large number of branches and tied them on to each other with pieces of

indweed and bryony, till nothing could be seen of either
f them among the leaves.

'Now what shall we do?' asked Grysslet, nervously.

'Just stay still,' answered the dragon. 'I shall practise
istening.'

So the patient Grysslet lay still under his canopy of
eaves and the dragon lowered his head and listened.

After about a quarter of an hour, he suddenly spoke.
You can't hear a dog barking, can you, Grysslet?'

'No,' said the knight, trying to find out which twig
t was that was sticking into his neck between his helmet
nd his armour. 'No, there's no dog barking.'

'I can hear one,' said the dragon. 'A curious bark – it
ounds almost like my name. Do keep still, Grysslet. I
an't hear it properly, you're rustling so. There it is again.
t's just like the words – *Dragon! Dragon! Dragon!*'

'Perhaps it's Wookey,' suggested Grysslet.

'It's nothing like his voice,' retorted the dragon. 'It's
ike a dog. I'm sure it's calling me.'

There was a long silence, broken only by the occasional
napping of a branch when Grysslet shifted uncom-
ortably.

'There it is again!' called the dragon, suddenly. 'It's
ery faint, but I can just hear it. "*Dragon!*" it called,
wice.'

Suddenly the branches over the dragon's face were
arted by a small brown hand, and Wookey peered into
is face.

'I've news,' he said. 'Bad news. Morgan le Fay has
rrived before us.'

Both Grysslet and the dragon shook some branches off
heir heads to hear better and the dwarf quickly told his
ale.

'I found the walls of the castle domain,' he said, 'and an old man led me towards the main entrance. When I got there, I found workmen, hammering away, trying to raise a stone pillar. The great iron gates were lying flat on the grass. On one side of the entrance was a stone gate post, with a carved beast on top of it, but the other, as say, was lying flat, and its beast had come off and was broken in pieces. I pretended I was a local farmer's son on my way to work, and I asked questions.

' "Yes, indeed," they told me. "The stone gate-post has come down and left the gate lying flat, and we are building it up again as fast as we can."

' "Who is it, then," I asked, "that goes round this countryside knocking down stone gate-posts?" But they couldn't answer.'

Deep was the gloom of the dragon and Sir Gryfflet. At last the knight suggested timidly: 'I suppose we couldn't go home to Camelot?'

'Home to Camelot!' exclaimed the dragon, shaking the last remaining leaves from his ears. 'Home to Camelot! Of course not. We've come to rescue David and rescue him we must. Wookey, while you were gone, I heard a voice, an odd voice rather like a dog's bark, calling "*Dragon! Dragon!*" Did you hear it at all?'

'A dog barking?' exclaimed Wookey. 'Yes, I did, and that old man who led me to the gates heard it, too. He asked the workmen if one of my lady's hounds was running loose. It was a hound's bark, he said. And he had heard it earlier that morning, when he was near the gates gathering firewood. "Very loud it was, then," he said. "There was a rumble of wheels down the road, and the hound barking." But then, of course, we began talking of the pillar and I didn't think of it again. Now,' said the dwarf, wrinkling his forehead, 'I begin to wonder if there is some connection. How does it all fit in?'

'I don't know,' answered the dragon. 'It's clear that Morgan le Fay has been there before us. And it looks as if she has managed to turn David back into himself from a stone gate-post, but *how*, when we've got her *Volume Two*?'

'I think I begin to see!' cried Wookey, in excitement. 'She can't turn him *back into himself*, without the book, any more than she can turn herself back, but she *can* turn him into *something else*, and that's what she's done. She's turned the gate-post into a hound, and taken it off in her coach. After all, she couldn't have taken a great stone pillar, could she? But she *could* take a dog. We must find out which way she's gone. After all, we've got her *Volume Two*. She can't go on forever turning David from one thing into another, and anyway, in the end she'll have to have the book, or else remain a hideous old witch herself for the rest of her life.'

They sat down, where they were, to work out a plan, Wookey, who had a great knowledge of geography and a strong bump of direction, spoke at last, drawing with his finger in the soft dust of the lane. 'We're here,' he said, making a mark in the dust. 'Here are mountains. I don't think she'll go there. In fact, I'm pretty certain she'll retrace her steps towards Camelot. She'll want to find us, as much as we want to find her. Let's get up on that small mound and survey the landscape. We are very near Castle Perilous indeed, and we don't want to get embroiled in the battle. You two had better wait here with Starlight and the charger. I'll go.'

Wookey was not long gone. He came back running. 'The battle is on!' he cried. 'Can't you hear it?' Faintly now, across the fields, they could hear the clash of swords. 'There are knights everywhere,' exclaimed Wookey, in great excitement.

At that moment there was a tremendous clatter and a tall knight came pounding down the road, in a cloud of dust, riding a massive bay charger.

'He's in red armour!' shouted the dragon. 'He's the Red Knight! Oh, where, where is Bewmains?'

He had hardly uttered the words, when there was a further clanking of armour, and down the lane came Bewmains, riding his charger at full gallop. He reined the horse in for a moment when he saw the dragon.

'Dragon!' he shouted. 'Did he come this way, the red villain, the russet fox?'

'He did! He did!' answered the dragon, blowing out clouds of green smoke in his fierce excitement. 'Ride on, on, Bewmains!'

It was too much for Wookey and the dragon. They could not bear to miss the combat, so, leaving Gryfflet to follow on his charger with Starlight and the provisions, they set off down the lane as fast as they could go. As they hurried on, the noise of battle grew louder and louder. There were horsemen fighting in every field. At last the towers of Castle Perilous loomed up before them, grey against the sky-line. A beautiful lady was leaning from one of the tower windows, and below, on the greensward, Bewmains and the Red Knight of the Red Lands were engaged in mortal combat. Just as the dragon and Wookey arrived, they leapt from their foaming horses, and drew their swords, and ran together like two fierce lions. Each gave the other such buffets upon his helmet that both knights reeled backwards. Then they recovered and hewed off great pieces of each other's armour, which fell in the field. They fought till they lost breath and stood staggering, panting, blowing and bleeding. Then they fell to battle again, hurling together like two rams, till they fell grovelling on the earth.

For a few moments they parted and sat down on two molehills to rest. They took off their helmets, and let the cool wind play on their heads. Bewmains looked up at the window and there he saw the fair Lady Lyonesse of the Castle Perilous. The sight of her spurred him on once more. He doubled his strokes and smote so thick that his sword fell out of his hand. Then he felled the Red Knight to the ground with one blow of his fist. Just at this moment, an extraordinary thing happened. Across the field came an elkhound, its tongue hanging out and its sides flecked with foam. It bounded up to the two knights, and planted its great tufted feet upon the chest of the Red Knight, just as Bewmains was pulling off the fallen

enemy's helmet and raising his sword to kill him. As
tonished, Bewmains held back. The elkhound whined and
gave little barks, and the dragon gave a bellow which
resounded down the field and echoed back from the walls
of the castle.

'It's David!'

The elkhound turned its head, and gave two deep
barks. And if ever a hound could speak, those barks cried
'Dragon! Dragon!' It bounded up to the dragon and
licked his scaly face, his long ears and his yellow horns.
It twisted in and out of his heavy paws, leapt over the
long finny tail, and all the time, its barking spelt only one
thing to the dragon. This was the voice he had heard
calling him from far away. All round, knights were laying
down their swords and spears, and dismounting from
their chargers to watch the extraordinary scene.

By now, Bewmains, his battle wrath having subsided,
had helped the Red Knight to his feet, and Lynette was
binding up their wounds, while the Lady Lyonesse had
come down from her castle window and was already
hurrying across the sward. The amazement of all at the
scene was suddenly changed to horror when, turning at
the sound of wheels, they saw a strange black coach,
rumbling and jolting across the field, and leaning from its
window, a hideous witch-like figure, waving her arms
and shrieking in blood-curdling tones at the top of her
voice. It was plain that some dreadful curse was being
uttered, though none could hear at first what she was
saying.

It was Wookey who acted quickly. Pulling the precious
Volume Two out of his wallet, he ran as fast as he could
towards the approaching carriage, waving the black book
as he went. At a word from Morgan le Fay (for of course

it was she) the coachman pulled up the horses, and the coach came to a standstill.

Wookey also stopped, and called out: 'Have you come for your elkhound or your *Volume Two*, my lady – or both?'

'Give it to me!' shrieked Morgan, clawing the air with her skinny fingers.

'Oh no, no, no!' answered Wookey, putting the volume quickly behind his back. 'You will have to do something to win it back.'

'Take it from him, coachman!' ordered the witch. 'Run him down! Drive the horses over him! Mince him to pieces under the wheels!'

The coachman did not move.

'Do as you are ordered!' she cried in a fury.

But Wookey was peering at the book, and he called out: 'I see there is a spell here, page seventeen, to be precise, which is headed "Spell for turning coachman back into a noble knight". That sounds useful.'

The coachman jumped down from his seat, ran to Wookey and shook him warmly by the hand.

'Twelve long months I've served her,' he groaned. 'Oh, if you'd only give me back my proper shape, I'd reward you with house and land, with a bag of gold, with –'

'Never mind the rewards,' said Wookey. 'You just remember the page number, seventeen.' He walked a little nearer the coach. Others were now crowding up behind him but the elkhound was whimpering, and sat between the dragon's paws with its tail between its legs, and the whites of its eyes showing.

Morgan le Fay was no longer shouting and blustering. She was sitting back on the seat of her coach, sulking and glowering. No one spoke. All were holding their breath

to hear what Wookey would say next. He was thumbing over the pages, looking for something.

'Ah!' he cried, at last. 'Here it is! I felt sure it must be here. "Elkhounds: useful spell for restoring elkhounds to original shape."'

Morgan le Fay bit her lips and said nothing. Wookey flicked over a page. 'Ah!' he cried. 'Here's one I think would interest you even more. "Old woman – hooked nose – skinny arms – wart on left cheek – spell for converting same to proper shape . . ."'

At these words, Morgan le Fay flung open the carriage door and made a rush at Wookey but the dwarf dodged quickly back, and two knights caught her as she tripped over a molehill. They held her fast, while Wookey looked calmly round him. 'The sun is going down,' he said. 'There are knights here whose wounds must be attended to, and all of us are weary and need our rest.' He looked sternly at Morgan le Fay. 'We are wasting time,' he went on. 'Either you perform these spells here and now, or I will throw your *Volume Two* into the big bonfire that you see yonder.'

Morgan le Fay swallowed her rage, and replied: 'Very well. I will perform them. Give me the book.'

'Ho! No!' cried Wookey, with a deep laugh. 'Ho! No, no, no! I am not being caught that way. Here are pages seventeen and twenty. You can have those first.' With that, he ruthlessly tore these two pages out of the little book and handed them to Morgan le Fay.

Trembling, she read through the recipe on page seventeen. 'I shall need the ingredients,' she said, 'or I shan't be able to perform the spell.'

'What are they?' asked Wookey, and peered over her shoulder. He read out loud:

'Juniper berries . . . twelve.

'A sprig of dead hawthorn and be sure the tree is withered and truly dead.

'A grey goose's feather . . .'

There was a moment's pause and then the Lady Lyonesse stepped out of the throng, and said that she could produce all three in no time. 'Page!' she called. 'There is a jar of juniper berries on the top right-hand shelf in the still-room. Fetch it this instant and bring, too, the quill pen from my writing desk, for that is made of a grey goose feather.' Then she turned to another page. 'Boy!' she cried. 'At the bottom of the field stands a dead thorn bush. Here, take my little penknife and go and cut a small branch of it.'

It was only a matter of moments before all three ingredients had been brought, and very unwillingly, with an extremely sour face, Morgan le Fay prepared her spell.

First she stuck a juniper berry on each thorn of the thorn twig. Then she took a flint and tinder box from her pocket and lit the dry branch. It flared up in an instant, and while it was burning, gradually wrinkling the juniper berries till they looked like black currants, she waved the goose feather three times slowly over the wisp of smoke and muttered:

> 'Lethera, hovera, dovera, dick!
> Coachman into knight – come quick!'

And before the astonished eyes of all, the red-faced, rather fat coachman changed into a tall, black-haired, pale-faced knight, with a fine shield emblazoned with his coat of arms, and a helmet from which waved a proud crest of feathers. With a cry of joy, Gryfflet, who had just ridden up on his charger, dismounted and ran towards the knight. It was his own brother Bertram whom he had supposed dead, killed on a quest he had been pursuing the previous year and from which he had never returned.

Wookey refused to allow their rejoicing to interrupt his work. 'Now,' he said, firmly, pushing Gryfflet and his brother to one side, 'let us turn to page twenty.'

The elkhound began to whine.

'Quiet! Good boy!' murmured the dragon, patting him absently while he listened to the spell which was to restore him to David, the giant cook.

'Take three leaves of meadow coltsfoot and squeeze from them the juice, smearing it upon the forehead of the bewitched person or creature. Then wave over its head from right to left seven times a peeled withy. Having done this, cause the afflicted party to eat a dog-biscuit soaked in red wine, and when all is done, repeat:

> Bothera, tothera, dothera, quirk!
> Coltsfoot, withy, do your work!'

The ingredients were fetched in no time, at the command of the Lady Lyonesse. The field was now quite silent, except for the whimperings of the elkhound. The creature's voice began to deepen as she waved the peeled withy over it, and when it had eaten the dog-biscuit soaked in wine, it began to grow. It stood upon its hind-legs, growing and growing, its sharp, pointed face filling out into roundness, its ears shrinking back into its head, and its brown hide changing into leather jerkin, leggings and boots. In a few moments, there stood before them the red-haired, cheerful giant cook, his face wreathed in smiles. He started to shake hands with everyone, beginning with the dragon and Gryfflet, and going on to Wookey, Bewmains, Gryfflet's new-found brother, the Red Knight, and the Lady Lyonesse and her sister. Then he proceeded to shake hands with everyone else he could see.

His hand-shakings were interrupted by the sour voice of Morgan le Fay. 'I suppose you look forward, you silly great booby, to going back to the kitchens at Camelot, and spending your life slaving in the grease and the smells? If you had obeyed me, you would have lived a life of idleness and wealth as a reward. Never mind, I still have your secret. *You still do not know who you are.* You simply know what once you were and what you will be again – a mere cook for the rest of your life.' With that she shrieked with evil laughter.

The dragon stepped forward. 'Madam,' he said politely. 'I do not think there will be any need for him to return to the kitchens at Camelot. *I know who he is.*' A hush fell upon the knights around, and Morgan le Fay stopped dead in the middle of a laugh. 'He is a royal giant,' went on the dragon. 'He is the son of King Jubeance and Queen Martha of the Black Forest.'

At these words, Morgan le Fay uttered a screech of quite a different kind. She looked wildly round her, realized that she now had no coachman to drive her, jumped on the seat of the coach, seized the reins herself, and with an unearthly 'He-e-e-up!' drove out of the field, the coach rattling and jolting, her black cloak streaming behind her in the wind.

'She has forgotten her *Volume Two*,' observed Wookey, quietly.

CHAPTER THIRTEEN

David Returns Home

BEWMAINS had accomplished his quest. He now intended to ride back to Camelot with the vanquished Red Knight of the Red Lands, accompanied by the Lady Lynette and her sister Lyonesse of the Castle Perilous. Wookey, of course, was anxious to get back to Ubley Warren, and the dragon wanted to restore the long-lost David to his giant parents, Jubeance and Martha.

Sir Gryfflet was very divided in his mind as to which party to join. As he walked up and down the meadow to cool his head after the feast, he argued with himself: 'Shall I go back to Camelot, with my dear brother? After all, we are of the same blood. He is younger than I am. It is my duty to escort him.' Then he sighed and argued the other side of the question: 'The dragon asked me to go on this quest with him. He has found the giant cook, it is true, but he has yet to get back to his parents. Who knows what adventures he may meet with on the way? I ought to go with him to protect him.'

Suddenly he heard a quiet voice from under an elder bush say: 'Silly old Gryfflet! I know what you are muttering to yourself. I can hear your thoughts quite clearly, they are so loud.'

Sir Grylflet started and looked round. From the branches glowed two yellow eyes. It was the dragon.

'What – what am I to do?' stammered Gryfflet.

'Go with your brother, of course,' answered the dragon. 'You have not seen him for a year, and if you join Bewmains' party, you will be quite safe going home and I shall not have to be anxious about you. Wookey and I will make our own way back with David, and before you know where you are, I shall be with you again at Camelot. And kindly see to it that the King has no more bad dreams about dragons, for I really cannot endure those smelly kitchens again.'

So the next day the two companies parted. Starlight, still carrying the provisions, went with Gryfflet and his brother, for the giant cook said he could obtain enough food for Wookey and the dragon and himself, 'And cook it, too,' he added. 'I'm an expert now. Oh, what will Mother say when she tastes my dumplings and hog puddens?'

The dragon and David had much to talk about, and Wookey, knowing this, dropped behind and said he had thoughts to think which would occupy him for some time. The two friends went over old times in the kitchen, of course. 'D'you remember?' they kept on saying to each other, and, 'I shall never forget when . . .' or, 'wasn't it funny that time . . .'

At last, the dragon decided to ask David the question he had been wanting to ask ever since he saw him again at Castle Perilous. 'David,' said the dragon, solemnly, 'there's something I want to ask you. Did you really try to poison the King and the court?'

David looked very uncomfortable. At last, after some minutes he said: 'It's no use. I can't lie to you. Yes, I *did* try to poison them – in a mild sort of way.'

'Mild!' exclaimed the dragon. 'I don't see that that makes it much better.'

'Well, I didn't kill anybody, did I?' retorted David, his great moon face looking rather sulky.

'No,' agreed the dragon. 'You didn't.'

'You don't understand, Dragon,' pleaded David. 'You don't understand the terrible position I was in.'

'You tell me, then,' said the dragon, sternly, 'and perhaps I shall understand how it was you were so kind as to try to poison everyone without killing them.'

'She brought me up,' began David.

'Morgan le Fay?'

'Yes, Aunt Mor, as I called her. She was very kind when she was in a good mood. She was strange too, strange because she was never the same. Sometimes old, sometimes young, sometimes ugly, sometimes beautiful. I never knew where I was with her.'

'Go on,' said the dragon.

After a pause, David continued: 'Aunt Mor was a witch. Did you know?'

'I was beginning to know,' said the dragon.

'She could do all sorts of spells, and she said she'd teach me some, if I would promise to do things for her. Of course I did. But she never taught me much, just silly little things.'

'Like you used to do in the kitchens,' suggested the dragon, 'to amuse the kitchen boys?'

'Yes,' said David. 'Rabbits out of hats and birds out of pies, and so on. I can't even remember the spells now.'

'A good thing,' interposed the dragon. 'The sooner you forget them the better. Go on.'

'One day she told me a long tale about her brother, Arthur, and how he had stolen the throne from her husband, Urience. Of course, I believed her, I'd no one else to believe, had I? She went on for a long time about Arthur and what a wicked king he was and how much hated by his subjects, who were, she said, longing to have good King Urience and good Queen Mor reigning over them happily ever after. She made me swear I would help her. She promised I'd be Lord Chancellor when her husband was king. Then, she laid her plot. I was to be a cook in Arthur's kitchens, and I was to poison the dishes.'

'And why didn't you succeed?'

David paused for a moment. 'When once I had lived in the kitchens,' he said, 'I found out how pleasant most people were. Of course, Sir Kay was a brute and the kitchen boys were often cheeky, but they weren't bad on the whole, and there was Bewmains.'

'Ah, he was a man in a thousand,' interrupted the dragon, glowing with pleasure at the very mention of the name.

'He was, he was. And there was you, too, Dragon.'

'You'd have had a job poisoning *me*,' remarked the dragon.

Looking around him as he spoke, he thought he could see, on the distant horizon, a thin, black line which might be the edge of the forest.

'Look! I believe we're nearly there!' he cried.

'We are,' called out Wookey, from behind them.

'I thought you were thinking secret thoughts,' said the dragon.

'Not all the time,' answered the dwarf. 'I've been
listening to your conversation between whiles, when I
thought it wasn't too private. Then, of course, I shut my
ears.'

'It wasn't ever really private,' said David, feeling
rather guilty that they had left the dwarf out of their talk.

'That's all right,' said Wookey, calmly. 'I listened to
most of it. Look – we've reached the border.'

In front of them was a large white stone on which was
carved: LAND OF THE BLACK FOREST.

The dragon was delighted to see the change that had
come over the fields since he had last seen them. Not a
sheep, not an ox was to be seen. Instead, every field was
standing deep in oats, blowing softly in the wind with
a pleasant rustling sound.

'Must be eating plenty of porridge,' commented the
dragon, with satisfaction and approval.

A few more miles and the Black Forest itself came into
sight and above it the towers of the castle. David gazed
at them, a slow recognition dawning in his face.

'Dragon!' he exclaimed. 'Do you know, I remember
this! Yes, I remember it all – The Black Forest and the
castle! I used to see it when I was a child. I often used to
dream about it and all the time it was my long-lost
home!'

He quickened his giant footsteps until even the dragon
found it difficult to keep pace with him, and they finally
arrived at the castle out of breath and trembling with
exhaustion. Knights came out and challenged them at the
gates, but they recognized the dragon at once, and treated
him with courtesy. 'You wish to have audience with
His Majesty?' they inquired.

'Audience, indeed!' snorted the dragon. 'It's King

Jubeance that will want to have audience with *me* when he hears what I've brought home to him.'

The knights were staring at the young red-haired giant, who was standing sheepishly behind the dragon.

'It's not...?' they cried. 'It can't be ...! You haven't...? Oh, my goodness! Fetch Their Majesties! Tell the King! Find the Queen!'

There was a clatter of armour, and a scurry of footsteps. Doors banged. Shouts echoed up and down the hall, and within a matter of seconds, King Jubeance came running through the archway, tearing down the sheepskin curtain in his hurry. Behind him came Queen Martha, her face red and crumpled with tears. In a moment, they were clasping their son to them, kissing him, shaking his hands, both of them talking at once, with the knights crowding round them, exclaiming as well, till the place was so noisy you would have fancied yourself in a farmyard of geese at feeding time.

By an extraordinary chance, they had arrived in the Land of the Black Forest on the eve of the giant cook's twenty-first birthday, which was Midsummer Day, 24 June. The midsummer festivities had never been held since David – or Giles, as he must now be called – had been stolen away, but once the first rejoicings were over, King Jubeance gave orders that the whole realm was to be given over to feasting for a fortnight. The dragon and Wookey, of course, were invited to stay, and while the dragon enjoyed the feast and the games and the jousting and trials of skill, the dwarf was very busy, filling notebook after notebook with details of giants and their way of life, to take back and put in the records at Ubley Warren.

At last, it was time for Wookey and the dragon to go

westward to the Mendips and Camelot. They said farewell to the giant king and his wife, and to Giles. A horse was given them, the smallest in the castle stables, but even he was like an out-sized cart-horse. He was laden with provisions, and presents, and at last, with many parting cries of 'Come and see us again!' and 'We'll never forget you!' they departed, rather exhausted by the festivities.

As they went, Wookey and the dragon talked of many things.

'I still have *Volume Two* of that wicked woman's spells,' said the dwarf. 'Will you take it back and give it to King Arthur? And will you ask him to make his villainous sister use it to turn back into their proper shape all those whom she has bewitched?'

'I will,' answered the dragon. 'She shall only have it back on that condition.'

As you will see, he carried out this request.

'I shall be sad to part from you,' said the dragon, looking gloomily at the little dwarf padding beside him, ten of his small steps going to one of the dragon's huge strides.

'You will always be welcome at Ubley, and it is not far from Camelot,' said Wookey.

'Ah, I doubt if I shall come that way again for some time,' answered the dragon, and sighed heavily. 'I do not wish to remain longer at Camelot. I have achieved my quest, and I have learned a great deal, but this life is not for me. I shall ask the King's permission to retire to Cornwall where I have a comfortable cave and many friends. It is now nearly two years since I saw them. They must wonder if I am still alive. If ever you are in Cornwall, Wookey, or any of your Ubley friends, come and visit me. My cave is at Constantine Bay, near the mouth of the

River Camel. It is a large cave and I could find sleeping quarters for several of you on rock ledges. There is much of scientific interest for you, besides – different kinds of rocks, you know, the ancient Cornish language, and other wonders such as mermaids.'

'I will certainly come,' said Wookey, with warm enthusiasm. 'We will make a special scientific expedition of it. I shall arrange it next year without fail.'

And then, as they saw the Mendips rising before them, and their roads were about to divide, the dwarf suddenly said: 'I have a special letter which I would like you to deliver to the King. Will you do this for me?'

'Certainly,' said the dragon.

'And there is a special letter for you, too,' went on Wookey, 'which you must not open till the King opens his. Will you promise?'

'I promise,' said the dragon, though he was consumed with curiosity.

Shortly after that, they parted with many hand and paw shakes. The dragon turned off to the left and Wookey to the right and soon they were out of sight of one another and travelling their ways alone.

CHAPTER FOURTEEN

The End of the Quest

IT was not long before the towers of Camelot came into sight, and it was with mixed feelings that the dragon saw them. Pleased though he was to be back, and to see old friends like Bewmains and Gryfflet again, he thought also of his long months in the kitchens. Suppose the King had another dream? thought the dragon. In any case I do not know that I am cut out for court life. Too many people. However, he was at least coming back successful, and as he entered the gates of Camelot, he blew out a few proud puffs of green smoke, and arched his long neck and curled his finny tail.

The King was out hunting, and many of his knights with him, but Bewmains was there, and Sir Gryfflet.

They greeted him warmly, and all sat down together in the sun on the castle battlements, to talk and await the King's return. During the conversation, Grffllet suddenly turned a bright pink and announced: 'I am going to be married.'

The dragon was very pleased. 'Just the thing for you,' he said. 'Now you can settle down, and enjoy life. By the way, has the King made you a member of the Round Table?'

'Not yet,' answered Gryfflet. 'He is waiting for your return and a full account of the quest. You don't ask "Who to?",' he added in rather disappointed tones.

'Who to what?' asked the dragon.

'Silly old Dragon,' said Bewmains. 'When someone says he is going to get married, you are expected to take an interest and ask the name of the lady.'

'Tut, tut!' said the dragon, blushing a little. 'I forget my manners. It's the result of long months of rough living. Dear Gryfflet, who is it? Tell me.'

'Her name is Morwenna,' answered Gryfflet, 'and she comes from Cornwall. I will introduce you to her this evening. She is very beautiful and – and – well, I like her very much,' ended the knight, rather bashfully.

'Splendid!' cried the dragon. 'She sounds just right. What about you, Bewmains?'

'Yes, as a matter of fact I am going to be married, too.'

'Not – not to the Lady Lynette?' asked the dragon, opening his eyes very wide.

'No, not to her, but to her sister,' answered Bewmains. 'To the Lady Lyonesse of Castle Perilous.'

'Ah,' said the dragon thoughtfully. More than ever, he realized that Camelot was no place for him. With his two best friends married, what use was there in his remaining? He looked rather sadly at them and sighed, but he said nothing. They felt that something was wrong and cheered him up with tales of all that had been going on at the court since they were away.

That evening, the King returned, and, in a crowded hall, the dragon approached him, knelt before him and told him the tale of his quest. The King and Queen and all the knights listened intently, and at the end Queen Guinevere embraced him and said she was proud of him. The Cornish knights cheered him, and Bewmains shook him by the paw. Only Sir Kay looked disagreeable and remarked: 'We have little proof, Your Majesty, that he has done all this.'

Bewmains looked angry. 'I was with him most of the time,' he said, 'and I can vouch for it.'

'*Most* of the time,' sneered Sir Kay. 'I should want more proof than that.'

'I was with him *all* the time,' cried Sir Gryfflet. 'Every word he says is true!'

'Perhaps,' said the dragon, politely, 'this letter will give His Majesty the proof he needs – if he needs it.' He then handed to Arthur the letter which Wookey had given him. It was not long. The King read it in silence and then passed it to Guinevere.

'May I read it to the court?' she asked.

'I think you may,' answered the King.

The Queen began to read.

Your Majesty,

In case there should be any doubt among you or your knights that this noble dragon has performed heroic deeds of endurance, and achieved the quest upon which he set out, I wish to state that I, Wookey, of the honourable company of

Mendip dwarfs to whom truth is the highest virtue, do swear that the dragon performed his quest as he set out to do, found and rescued the giant cook, David, and restored him safe and sound to his parents, King Jubeance and Queen Martha, of the Land of the Black Forest.

The dragon has in his possession a book of spells belonging to your sister, Morgan le Fay. He will explain to you the full wickedness of this woman, and I trust that Your Majesty will treat her as she deserves.

Your loyal servant,
Wookey.

Now, the dragon had not mentioned Morgan Le Fay's name, nor spoken of *Volume Two* of the spells. He intended to tell the King about it privately, thinking that he might not be pleased to have his sister, even if she was only his half-sister, shown up in front of all the court as a wicked witch, with a fondness for poisoning people. But now the truth had been told for him. The King turned pale. For a few moments he said nothing, but his hand gripped the arm of his chair so tightly that the knuckles went white. The dragon watched the King's hand. Slowly the muscles relaxed, and then Arthur spoke: 'We will consider the matter of my sister Morgan le Fay in a moment,' he said, speaking very quietly. 'Now we have something pleasanter to do. Noble Dragon of Cornwall, with my sword I dub thee knight. Rise, Sir Dragon!'

The dragon felt the King's sword touch him lightly on each scaly shoulder. He rose to his feet amid the cheers of the knights, and bowing to the King, thanked him humbly for this high honour.

The King then looked sternly round him. 'Where is my sister, Morgan le Fay?' he demanded.

Her wretched husband, Urience, who had been out

hunting with the King, stepped forward. 'She is at home,'
he said, miserably.

'At home!' cried the King. 'I thought she was still
in – where was it? – Wales?'

'No, Your Majesty,' said the unhappy Urience. 'She
came back some days ago, but she is – she is not quite
herself. She has remained shut up in her room ever since,
and sees no one.'

'Indeed,' said Arthur. 'She is going to see me. Fetch
her immediately.'

Messengers were despatched and great was the amazement of the King and the whole court when they returned

with an ugly old witch, who bore no resemblance to the Morgan le Fay that the King knew.

The story of the Book of Spells, *Volume Two*, was soon told, and the dragon handed it to the King who turned over the pages until he came to page twenty-nine.

'Old woman – hooked nose – skinny arms,' he read. 'Spell for converting same to proper shape.'

Slowly he tore the page out of the book, and folded it up. 'Morgan le Fay,' he said, solemnly. 'Here is your book. Go to your stillroom, and brew all those spells necessary for restoring to their proper shape any of my unfortunate subjects whom you have bewitched. Only when you have done this, will I return to you this page, and allow you to restore yourself to your own person.'

In silence, Morgan took the book. Casting a furious look at the dragon, who smiled back politely, she left the hall, clutching the little black volume.

The King put page twenty-nine into a leather wallet at his side. He then looked at the dragon for a moment.

'Noble Sir Dragon,' he said at last. 'It remains to find some position for you in my household, and some apartment where you may live.'

The dragon cleared his long, green throat. 'I am thinking of returning to Cornwall,' he said.

There was a loud outcry at this. The Cornish knights, in particular, made a great clamour, but the dragon checked them with his paw.

'I miss the sea,' he said, simply. 'I miss my own cave, and the rocks, and the starlit nights, and my old friends. Let me return to Cornwall, Sir King. When you hold court at Tintagel, I will visit you there, and take my part in court life for a time, but I am a dragon of plain habits, and prefer my cave to a king's palace.'

'You shall do as you wish,' said Arthur, 'but tonight we will give a feast in your honour. Tomorrow you shall go home, with an escort of Cornish knights beside you.'

During the feast that evening a herald announced that a stranger sought audience with the King. He was ushered in, a rough fisherman in a sea-stained jersey. In his hands he held a bottle, and he explained that he had found it on the shore (Camelot is not far from the sea), and thought it best to bring it to the King.

'It be addressed to zome dragon,' he said, 'and I do know no dragons, but thought the proper place for they be a king's court, so here 'tis.'

'The dragon is behind you,' said the King, with a smile.

The fisherman gave a jump, and turning round, saw the dragon's yellow horns and green head on the opposite side of the table.

'A zee-zerpent be nothing to un!' he muttered, staring hard, as he handed the bottle over.

If the dragon had been in any doubt about going back to Cornwall, the letter in the bottle would have decided him. It was from Harry, the lobster-man, to whom the dragon himself had sent a message in a bottle when he was in London at the King's wedding. The dragon almost wept as he read it. It brought back to him the smell of the sea, and the feel of the spray blowing into his cave in the rough weather, the moonlit rocks, and all the things about Cornwall he had missed so much since he had left nearly two years before.

Dear frend draggon, [said the letter]
    We do miss ee very much. We do not know as how a cort is a place for a draggon and hopes you will come soon back

to us volk in Constantine Bay. We keep our eye on yor cave.
It is all zafe and zound, dontee worrit.

Harry.

P.S. Yor letter was washed up last week.

The dragon handed the paper over to the King who
read it and said, quietly: 'I see. Yes, Sir Dragon, I think
you are right. You should return. But next spring, I shall
hold my court in Tintagel Castle, and then we shall meet
again.'

So next day, the dragon set out with his escort. Sir
Gryfflet had insisted on being one of them, much to the
dragon's pleasure. He felt it was very unselfish of the
knight to leave his beautiful young lady, and told him so.

'I am fonder of you than anyone else – except, of course,
Morwenna,' said the knight.

It was not till they were out on the road to Cornwall
that the dragon remembered that he had not yet opened
the letter which Wookey had given him for himself. In
the excitement of being knighted and eating a special
feast in his honour, and getting the message from Harry
the lobster-man, he had altogether forgotten it. Hastily he
tore it open. Inside was a small piece of paper on which
was written:

Dear Dragon,

You are now a Listener of the First Order. You could hear
the speech of the bats, in Lammock's Lair, and the barking of
the elkhound, from miles away. As High Master of the Mendip
Order of Listeners, I am going to give you a secret name. This
name you may give only to your closest friends. If ever they
are in trouble, they must call this name, and you will hear it,
and come to their aid.

I shall miss you,
Wookey.

At the bottom of the letter was a name. What that name is cannot be written in this tale for it is told by the dragon only to his closest and dearest friends. It begins with an R and no one who calls it will call in vain, for so powerful is its magic that it will reach the dragon's ears, no matter where he is.

The end of The Dragon's Quest

The Book is Finished

SUE had reached the end of *The Dragon's Quest*. Her head was tired with the effort of reading and she suddenly noticed that the light in the cave was rather dim, and that she was extremely hungry. Goodness! she thought. I must have been here for hours. I do hope Mummy and Daddy haven't been worried. She rose to her feet rather stiffly to put the book back on its rock shelf and as she did so, she hesitated for a moment. The sea sounded very near, horribly near. Still clutching the book, Sue ran to the entrance of the cave, her fears growing. Yes, there it was, right across the sands in front of her – the heaving, dark-grey sea, stretching across the tiny cove only a few feet away from the entrance to the cave. She was cut off! Afraid, she looked round her, to see if she could climb the rocks by the cave itself, and reach the cliff-top, but their black, steep surfaces gave no foothold.

'Whatever shall I do? Oh, whatever shall I do?' she cried to herself. Then she remembered the dragon's motto – *Dragons Never Despair!* 'I won't be frightened,' she said firmly to herself. 'I'll call for help and someone will be sure to come.'

So she stood at the mouth of the cave, with the sea only a few feet away from her, and started to shout as loud as she could: 'Help! Help! I'm cut off!' But her voice wasn't strong enough to carry above the noise of the waves. She called again and again till her throat ached, but she heard no answering shout from the cliff top above her. Then sitting down on a rock in misery and despair, she found she was still holding the book of *The Dragon's Quest*, and she clutched it to her and wept. 'Oh, Dragon, dear Dragon, I *do* wish you were here!'

The sea gave a sudden roar at that moment, and heaved itself a foot nearer to her across the strip of sand that was all there was left of the cove. 'Dragon! Dragon!' it seemed to be growling at her, and then – 'Call him! Call him!' it urged.

She rubbed her hand over her wet eyes and jumped up, almost laughing. 'How stupid I am!' she cried. 'Of course I can call him. I know he'll come. He's *sure* to come!'

Turning her face to the sea, she cupped her hands over her mouth and cried, as loudly as she could, the dragon's name that began with an R, the secret name that only she and Sir Gryfflet and a very few others had ever known.

She called it three times, and three times more. Then she stood and gazed out to sea, over the rising tide. Something small and black, like a sea-bird, was flying over the horizon. Nearer and nearer it came, growing bigger and bigger, and even before she could recognize him, she knew it was the dragon. A minute more and there was a loud splash! He had landed in the water at the edge of the waves and, shaking his scales dry, was hurrying towards her.

'Oh, my claws and fins!' he exclaimed. 'That was a near one! Never flew so fast in all my life! Whatever were you doing to get cut off? My scales and smoke! You might have been drowned, you foolish girl!'

Sue hugged the dragon and started to scramble on to his back. 'Take me home,' she whispered.

'I'd better,' said the dragon. 'The water is nearly up to my ankles as it is.' He blew out a puff of green smoke, beat his wings slowly and rose in the air over the cliff-top.

'There are Mummy and Daddy!' cried Sue. 'They're looking for me!'

Below her, she could see her anxious father and mother hurrying along the cliff-top and peering over. The dragon made an elegant landing just behind them and Sue ran to them, calling out, 'I'm safe! I'm safe!'

They were too relieved and happy to ask for explanations, but Sue wanted to tell them what had happened.

'I was cut off!' she cried, breathlessly. 'I was reading in the dragon's cave down there and the sea came up into the cove. But I called the dragon's name, and he rescued me at once. He's here, look!'

She turned and pointed towards the dragon – but he had disappeared. Her mother and father took her by the hand

and began to walk back along the cliff-top, but Sue pulled away from them and looked over her shoulder. She could see the dragon now, flying away in a westerly direction, his green figure growing smaller and smaller. And then she saw that he had blown her a kiss in green smoke, just as he used to do in the old days. It hung in the air for several minutes, and then slowly faded into the evening clouds.

About the Author

Rosemary Manning was born in Dorset in 1911. After taking a Classics Degree, she has had a varied career in business, teaching, and lecturing, though she would describe her main profession as that of writer. In addition to five children's books, she has written several novels for adults and a number of short stories. She now lives for much of the year in the West Country, which she knows well and uses as the setting for many of her books, including *Green Smoke* and *Dragon in Danger*. (also published in Puffins.)

Also by Rosemary Manning

GREEN SMOKE

R. Dragon was 1,500 years old, and he had a great partiality for almond buns. He was a dragon with impeccable manners, who was far too polite to eat people and he avoided meeting them because he did not like frightening them. He could also tell stories, and Sue heard about the Cornish giants and fairies, and of King Arthur whom he had known very well. He taught Sue songs and took her to tea with a mermaid, who told her about the country under the sea.

Altogether a charming 'someone' to discover, as boys and girls from six to nine will find out for themselves.

DRAGON IN DANGER

It was nearly the end of Sue's second holiday in Cornwall, where her good friend R. Dragon had lived ever since the days of King Arthur.

The green dragon was very sad to think Sue was going so soon. She was the first human friend he had had for hundreds of years, and he was going to miss her. Then he had an idea – he would visit Sue in *her* home in St Aubyns.

But Sue was worried about it. How would he get there? And where could he live? Not in her little house, for sure. Well, one way and another R. Dragon got over those difficulties, and he was soon nicely settled on an island in St Aubyns, and was even invited to take the star part in the local pageant. But wicked Mr Bogg and Mr Snarkins began to plot against him.

If you have enjoyed this book and would like to know about others which we publish, why not join the Puffin Club? You will receive the club magazine, *Puffin Post*, four times a year and a smart badge and membership book. You will also be able to enter all the competitions. For details send a stamped addressed envelope to:

The Puffin Club, Dept. A
Penguin Books Limited
Bath Road
Harmondsworth
Middlesex